NO 

A Bridge City Beats NOVELLA

STEPHANIE LOUISE

Contents

Dedication   V

1. Kyla   1

2. Adam   18

3. Kyla   42

4. Adam   53

5. Adam   63

6. Kyla   73

7. Adam   77

About the Author   86

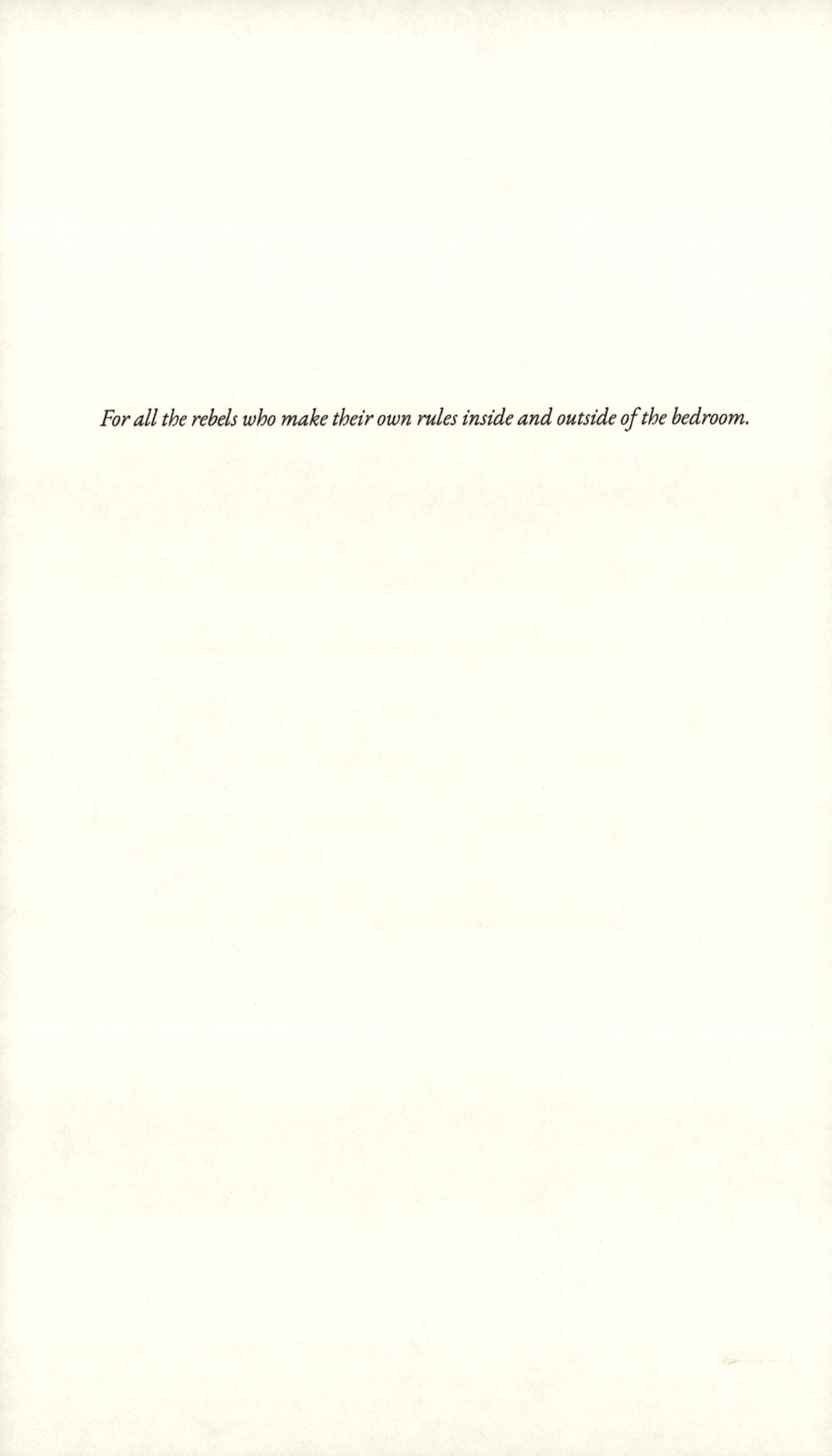

For all the rebels who make their own rules inside and outside of the bedroom.

I

Kyla

Kyla glanced at the clock on her car stereo. "Shit."

Her cousin Charlotte's wedding started in forty-five minutes, and she still hadn't reached her exit.

Kyla was *never* late to her commitments, but the morning hadn't gone as planned. A Labrador, Barkley Boo, was brought into the clinic at seven after ingesting half a bag of chocolate chips. The head veterinarian was stuck in traffic, so Kyla had to take a quick detour on her way to the wedding to treat the sick pooch. As the clinic's only intern and with half the staff out with the flu, she had no choice.

She was stressing on the entire drive from Corvallis, knowing there was no way she'd make it in time for the morning rehearsal. She'd never been in a wedding before, but how hard could it be to link arms with a groomsman and walk down an aisle? The wedding planner could probably fill her in on when to walk and where to stand so she didn't look like a clueless moron.

Luckily, Kyla's bridesmaid dress wouldn't take long to slip into, and her hair looked fine. A swipe of lipstick and a little eyeshadow would have her ready enough for wedding photos. She hit her blinker, taking the first exit for the Columbia Gorge. Ten minutes later, she was pulling up to the wrought iron gates of the Fairy Falls Inn.

A beef castle of a man in head-to-toe black clothes stepped to her window. "ID, please."

"Oh." Kyla blinked. "Okay." This was the first celebrity wedding she'd attended and probably the last, so the security check caught her off guard. But it made sense. Charlotte's punk band, Killing Daisies, had a top-ten album, and she was marrying one of the biggest rockstars on the planet—of course they'd want to keep out the paparazzi and crazy fans. Kyla dug through her purse and tugged the driver's license from her wallet.

The man's eyes slid from her face to the ID and back again before returning it. "Enjoy the wedding, Ms. Ross."

After parking in the gravel lot, Kyla grabbed her dress and heels from the backseat and sprinted toward the entrance. In the lobby, the receptionist at the massive oak desk greeted her with a smile while chatter from other areas of the inn echoed off the stone walls.

"Welcome to the Fairy Falls Inn." The receptionist's eyes slid to the dress in Kyla's hand. "The other bridesmaids are getting ready in the Trillium Room." She gestured to a long hallway off the lobby.

"Thank you." As Kyla turned in that direction, the warm, rich scent of coffee called to her. *Hollered* was more like it. There wasn't time to get a proper caffeine fix before work, so she followed the scent to grab a cup to chug while she got ready.

Just past the receptionist's desk, a large table was set up with a breakfast spread that was a coffee and pastry lover's dream—Kyla was both. Her stomach growled at the heavenly scents of vanilla, butter, and sugar in the air. Watching a forty-pound dog barf up a bellyful of brown foam had killed her appetite for breakfast, but now, it was back with a vengeance.

She glanced at her watch. Time was short, but there was enough for a quick bite. She set her heels on the ground and draped her dress over one arm while deciding what she wanted. It didn't take long—one of her favorites sat at the center of a doily-lined plate.

As she reached for the last bear claw, a male hand snatched it before she could.

"Shit," Kyla mumbled under her breath. She looked at the other offerings and decided to go with a croissant. Second best, but still great.

"Did you want this?"

Kyla's chin raised to look at the bear claw snatcher, and her response caught in her throat.

He was tall and broad-shouldered, his hair spiked and dark, the same color as the coffee she craved. The edges of tattoos crawled up his neck beneath the collar of his shirt, and his eyebrow was pierced with a silver ring. The tuxedo he wore looked expensive, giving him an air of sophistication that warred with the dirty, sexy punk he clearly was beneath it all.

A corner of his mouth hitched up, and his eyes gave her a slow, thorough perusal that left her craving something else. Even though she was in faded jeans and the vintage Rolling Stones T-shirt she'd worn under her lab coat at work, he obviously liked what he saw.

"Yeah," Kyla said, clearing her throat and shaking off the feeling. Mostly. "But you were faster and got it fair and square."

He stepped closer, encroaching on her personal space and hitting her with the scent of musky cologne that would smell really nice on her sheets. She licked her lips, and he tracked the movement, his jaw tensing.

"I'm not always so fast," he said, his pierced eyebrow lifting. "Slow's nice, too."

Holy hell.

Heat rose to her cheeks. Kyla didn't know what to say to that and really needed to get ready, so she turned to the table, filled a cup with coffee, and grabbed a croissant.

The guy swiped the pastry from her hand and bit it, his jaw moving as he watched the confusion cross her expression. A small crumb was left on his lip, and his teeth slowly dragged it inside his mouth before he dropped the croissant on the table. Somehow, he made even the simple act of chewing appear suggestive, and it was impossible to look away. Without warning, he captured her wrist, setting the bear claw onto her palm. His thumb brushed across her skin before he let her go.

"The carbs would go straight to my thighs anyway," he said.

She let out a burst of nervous laughter that died when he leaned closer.

"Besides," he said with another agonizingly slow eye fuck that made her pulse race. "I like making sure ladies get what they really want."

Kyla couldn't hold back the tiny gasp, and a slow smile of satisfaction ate up his face.

"Thanks," she whispered. It came out breathy, and she felt ridiculous.

She was all worked up over some guy handing her a goddamn *pastry*?

Kyla probably looked pathetically desperate and hard up for a hard-on. Sadly, it wasn't untrue. Between her finals at Oregon State and her internship, it had been a hectic, exhausting year. It'd been almost five months since she got laid, though it hadn't really bothered her until that moment. Sex was great, but she had plenty of toys at home to keep her satisfied enough.

But toys couldn't pin her to a mattress or kiss her until her lips were bruised.

An ache of need bloomed between her legs at his scent, suggestive words, and those dangerously beautiful brown eyes that were hazy with lust and a dirty, unspoken invitation.

"What's your name?" he asked.

Any other time and place, and she'd be all over this guy like sprinkles on a donut. He was excellent one-night stand material—bold, hot as sin, with a confidence bordering on cocky that was likely well-deserved.

But today, Kyla had other priorities than tending to her libido. She was there to help ensure her cousin's wedding was perfect and didn't need a distraction, no matter how nice that distraction was to look at.

Time to shut this shit down.

"Sorry." Kyla tore her eyes from his and shoved aside the dirty thoughts, shifting back into bridesmaid mode. "Whatever this was has been fun, but I'm already late and need to get ready."

She sipped her coffee, wincing at the bitterness. Her eyes roamed the table before she noticed he was standing in front of the sugar bowl. Of course.

"Excuse me," she said, gesturing with her cup.

The guy stepped back, and she added a spoonful of sugar to her coffee, stirring it in as he watched. "You're Charlotte's cousin, right?"

Since asking how he knew that would invite more conversation and make her even later, Kyla just nodded. She bit into the bear claw, nearly groaning as the sweet cinnamon-dusted perfection hit her tastebuds.

"What's your name?" he asked again.

Kyla swallowed the bite she'd taken and sighed, wishing he'd disappear and wishing he'd move closer at the same time. He smelled more edible than anything on the table, and the attention was nice. Still, she had a job to do. He'd probably forget all about her in five minutes anyway.

"Look," she said, "you're hot and all, but I'm here for my cousin. I'm sure you'll have no problem finding some other girl to succumb to your impressive and obviously well-practiced charms."

That was kind of harsh, but she needed him to buzz off before she did something reckless like ask about his tattoos or lick his mouth.

"Ouch." He laughed, the sound a low, gravelly rumble. "Shooting me down already? We were just getting started."

"Afraid so." Kyla chugged half her coffee, the glorious caffeine jolt warming her blood. "And *we* weren't starting anything. I was starving and needed coffee, and you..." She trailed off, unsure how to finish the thought. She wasn't often at a loss for words, but his presence was disorienting.

"I... what?" His sly smile grew.

She groaned and took another bite, frustrated by his teasing but still annoyingly drawn to his flirty, playful energy. "Whatever. You know what I'm talking about."

A woman around their age with blonde hair to her waist and a curve-hugging black dress walked to the receptionist's desk carrying a glass of champagne. The woman was model-gorgeous, but surprisingly, the guy's head didn't turn.

"If you're really not interested," he said, "what's the harm in telling me your name?"

"No harm, but also no point." Kyla lifted her bear claw toward the woman, whose tight figure said she'd probably never touched a pastry in her life. "I bet *she'd* love to tell you her name."

He glanced over, his expression unchanging, before returning his attention to Kyla. "I don't give a shit what her name is. I asked for yours."

Kyla's pulse ticked in her neck as she downed the rest of her coffee and tossed the cup into the trash. "Sorry, the answer's still no. And I really need to get changed."

He rubbed the stubble darkening his chin and cheeks as he watched her. His scrutinizing gaze made her feel strangely exposed but not uncomfortable. Instead, she was curious about what he was looking for.

"Okay." A side of his mouth pulled up in another lopsided grin. "Don't let me stop you, sweetheart." He picked up her shoes by their straps, holding them out.

"Thanks." She took the shoes, careful to avoid contact with his skin.

His eyes flicked to her dress. "If you need help zipping or unzipping anything, let me know."

I know something I'd like to unzip.

Kyla bit her bottom lip as the unwelcome thought invaded her mind, trying like hell not to picture him naked but failing miserably. Even in a tuxedo, she could tell he was well-built and firm. She was a sucker for inked muscles. After her bridesmaid duties were over, would it be so wrong to sneak away for a few hours of naughty fun with a handsome stranger?

They stood inches apart, neither of them speaking. The sexual tension thickened in the air, and her mind flashed with images of him with his shirt off and her on her knees, taking his—

"Kyla!" Charlotte ran over in her gorgeous white silk wedding gown and hugged her tight. "I'm so glad you made it."

"Hey, cuz." Kyla hugged her back, holding the rest of her bear claw a safe distance from the white dress. "Sorry I'm late. You look beautiful. Are you ready for this?"

Charlotte grabbed a few blueberries from a dish on the table and popped them into her mouth. "As my almost-husband would say, abso-fucking-lutely."

Kyla turned to where the sexy stranger had been standing, but he was gone as quickly as he'd appeared. She looked around the lobby, coming up empty.

"Who was that guy?" Kyla asked.

Charlotte shook her head, a disapproving frown replacing her smile. "Nope. Bad news. I love that boy, and while I'd trust him with my life, I wouldn't trust him with my dear cousin's lady bits."

The tingling heat in Kyla's belly said that her lady bits weren't interested in Charlotte's buzz-killing opinion.

"Why not?" Kyla bit into her bear claw and chased it with a mouthful of coffee. "He's hot as all hell. Lord knows I could use a tension release. Is he single?"

Charlotte scoffed. "Chronically. Trust me, honey, he's a player, and so is his sidekick, Zack, who'll probably try to get in your pants, too."

Kyla didn't need a commitment when she lived over an hour away, so the player thing didn't bother her. And that meant he had experience, so he'd know how to hit all the right buttons. What would be the harm in a little no-strings action before heading back to her long work hours, empty apartment, and not nearly enough fun?

"Is Zack as cute as that one?" Kyla aimed a thumb at where the guy had been standing. "What was his name anyway?"

"Yeah, Zack's cute as fuck too." Charlotte's shoulders dropped as she exhaled through her nose. "And his name's Adam. He's the drummer in Ty's band, and Zack plays bass."

Kyla's jaw unhinged before snapping shut.

The cute guys were *musicians*?!

Since dating a guitarist in high school, Kyla had a thing for creative guys, especially musicians. They were often more passionate and in touch with their feelings. And they had strong hands from all that pounding and fingering—on instruments, that is. But maybe if the night went her way, on her body too.

"Damn." Charlotte rolled her eyes. "I can see it all over your face. He's already got his hooks into you."

"It's not his hooks I'm interested in." Kyla grinned and got another eye roll.

"I've gotta hand it to the guy, he works fast." Charlotte popped some more blueberries. "They're the type that bail after everyone gets their rocks off. Don't say I didn't warn you."

Kyla's eyebrow arched. "They?" *Everyone?*

"Fucking hell, girl." Charlotte grabbed Kyla's shoulders. "They often work together. Threesomes. The girls leave their rooms smiling but end up hurt when they turn cold afterward and move on to the next one."

Kyla's excitement deflated like a slashed tire.

Threesomes? No. That wouldn't work. While the idea intrigued her, and she'd like to try it someday, Kyla was a planner. If she was going to do something that adventurous, she needed to know long beforehand to mentally prepare herself. And physically. Did she miss a spot shaving? She couldn't even remember if, in her rush to get out the door, she'd put on granny panties or something nicer.

And there were other factors to consider. While she was far from being a virgin, what if she wasn't exciting or skilled enough to keep two guys with a lot more experience satisfied? What if they were too rough and hurt her? Or what if they took one look at her curvy hips and soft stomach and changed their minds? What if the experience ended up being more embarrassing than fun?

A night of casual sex would send her home happy and recharged for the week ahead, but this was more complicated than a one-night stand with a hot stranger. Could she handle something that far outside her comfort zone?

"I'm telling you," Charlotte continued, "they're bad news. If you want some post-reception fun, my bassist Luke could show you a good time. He's sweet and funny, and he'd actually call if you gave him your number. Adam would take it and use the paper to spit his gum into."

Kyla thought about all of that as she chewed the last bite of her pastry. So, there was a safer option. Safer was good. Right?

She'd be sure to check out this Luke, but the feel of Adam's thumb stroking her wrist still lingered on her skin. The way he'd checked her out said he appreciated what she had on offer and would happily join her for a few hours of innocent fun.

Although, she could tell that *nothing* about that boy was innocent.

Too bad he was looking for more than she could handle.

"I'm here for you," Kyla assured her cousin. "I won't let you down by getting distracted by hot dudes. Even though they're hot *musicians,* and I've been in a serious sex drought."

Charlotte waved a dismissive hand as she laughed. "Don't worry about me. Just let loose and have fun. I know how hard you work, and Sandra and Amber will happily pick up your slack if you hit it off with Luke. Or anyone else who isn't Adam or Zack." Charlotte glanced at the clock on the wall and let out a happy shriek. "I'm getting married in fifteen minutes! Get dressed and meet us behind the double doors leading outside." She grabbed another handful of blueberries and disappeared behind a heavy wooden door off the lobby.

Time was too short to hunt down the Trillium Room, so Kyla found a bathroom and slipped into her dress and heels. She fluffed the loose waves of her long, dark locks in the mirror and put on a little gray eyeshadow and soft pink lipstick. She gave her reflection a nod. She didn't look as made-up as she'd planned before the call from work derailed her morning, but she looked pretty enough for photos and bridesmaid duties.

Kyla went back through the lobby and into the room where Charlotte had gone. Near the doorway, a woman in a business suit held a clipboard, going over something with a guy in a caterer uniform. That must be the wedding planner. Kyla needed to ask who she was walking with and when, but she didn't want to disturb their conversation. She looked around while waiting for an opportunity to speak.

Charlotte's arm was hooked with her dad, Mickey's, as they stood at the back of a line of people who were all paired up—except one person.

Adam.

Was Kyla supposed to walk up with *him*? Their arms would be touching. And the scent of his sexy cologne would probably cling to her skin after they parted.

The idea made her shiver.

"Kyla!" Uncle Mickey beckoned her over.

In her peripheral vision, she saw Adam's shoulders stiffen and his head swivel toward her.

"Hey, Ky." Sandra smiled from the front of the line. Aside from being the lead singer of Charlotte's band, Sandra had been best friends with Charlotte since grade school, so Kyla had hung out with her a lot over the years. Sandra was impossible not to love.

Amber stood behind Sandra, her head turning. "Glad you made it, Kyla. You look great." They'd only met twice before, backstage at Killing Daisies shows, but while she played tough, it was clear the beautiful blonde drummer was just as sweet as her friends.

"You look stunning, sweetheart." Uncle Mickey released Charlotte's arm to hug Kyla and give her a peck on the cheek. He was her favorite uncle, and when she was growing up, he'd taken her and Charlotte camping on Mount Rainier every summer. They'd hike, and he'd tell them ghost stories around the fire. He was stern and tough on the outside but had a big, soft heart.

"Thanks, Uncle Mickey." Kyla pulled back and noticed that her cousin looked conflicted—her eyes darted around the room, her lips pursed. It was surprising to see minutes before Charlotte was marrying the love of her life. "You okay, cuz?"

Charlotte shook off the expression and gave her dad a reassuring grin. "Of course! Happiest day of my life." She wrapped both hands around Kyla's bicep and, with slow, reluctant steps, guided her to stand beside Adam.

He stopped talking to the almost-as-cute guy paired up with Amber and turned to them.

"Hello again." A grin inspired by the devil himself greeted her. "Looks like you're stuck with me."

Charlotte smacked his arm. "Behave yourself, Adam." She pointed at the guy beside Amber. "Both of you. Don't make me have to open a can of whoop-ass on my wedding day."

"What did I do?" The guy with Amber snickered. "I'm just standing here."

Charlotte scoffed before returning to her dad.

Kyla felt the heat of Adam's gaze as she focused on the back of Amber's blonde head. She was afraid to be pulled back into the hypnotizing look of lust that seemed so effortless and natural to him, it was probably a permanent feature. Their shoulders bumped, but she knew damn well it wasn't an accident.

"Hey, Zack." Adam's eyes stayed on the side of her face. "Meet Kyla."

"Bear Claw Girl?" The voice in front of them had dropped an octave and positively dripped with sex. Zack turned his head, giving her the same head-to-toe sweep Adam had. His almost-black hair was long enough to grab, but just barely. The eyes shamelessly checking her out were a deep shade of green with flecks of honey along their rims. This close, she could see the faint shadow of dark stubble on his cheeks, giving his cleaned-up look a sexy, dangerous edge.

Being on the receiving end of their hungry looks sparked a needy ache between her legs. Her thighs squeezed together, reflexively chasing a pressure release, and the low chuckle beside her said Kyla hadn't been as subtle as she'd thought.

Finding out she'd been nicknamed because of her taste in pastries shouldn't be nearly as arousing as Zack's voice. But it wasn't the name—it was the fact that Adam had talked to him about her. She exhaled a slow breath, wishing she'd been a fly on the wall for that conversation. Considering what Charlotte said about them sharing women and how Zack was still staring at her like a tiger about to pounce, she had a pretty good idea of what they talked about.

"Yup." Adam nodded beside her.

"You were right," Zack said.

With that, her hair whipped against her cheek as she turned to Adam. As expected, that heated gaze he did so well instantly drew her in.

Her cousin was right. This boy was bad fucking news.

Moth, meet flame.

"Right about what?" Kyla asked, her voice obnoxiously breathy again. She prided herself on the ability to maintain her composure under pressure, but somehow Adam made it impossible to keep her shit together.

How did this guy keep throwing her off her axis so easily?

"Get to your places, please," the wedding planner called out.

"Don't worry about it, sweetheart." His arm slid into the crook of Kyla's elbow. Again, his intoxicating scent hit her, and again, her thighs squeezed together like she was trying to put out the fire he'd ignited between them. His widening grin said he'd caught that one, too.

The wedding planner propped open the doors.

The sounds of an acoustic guitar filled the air. It was a beautiful tune, perfect for the occasion. Kyla focused on the song instead of the delicious distraction beside her.

"That's our cue." The wedding planner gestured to Tyler's brother, Matthew, and Sandra to go out first. They slowly made their way down the aisle, where Tyler and the minister waited.

"Another one bites the fucking dust," Zack said, followed by a grunt of pain.

Amber had stomped his foot. "That's what you get."

Kyla liked her. The girl had spunk.

When Sandra and Matthew were about halfway down the aisle, Amber and Zack stepped forward. The wedding planner was chatting up the caterer again, and Kyla started to panic.

"Shit," she murmured.

Adam turned. "What's wrong?"

"I missed the rehearsal. I don't know when we're supposed to go out, how slow we go, or where I stand."

His fingertips ghosted over her arm, triggering a wave of goosebumps. "Just follow my lead. I got you." He stepped forward once Amber and Zack started down the aisle, and Kyla followed. "When we get up there, you'll go to Amber's right."

Kyla nodded, feeling a little better. "Thanks."

The last thing she wanted was to fuck up and draw attention to herself when Charlotte deserved the spotlight. She appreciated his reassurance. Apparently, even skirt-chasing players could be polite.

"Any time, Bear Claw Girl." His hand stroked the bare skin of her forearm again before it dropped to his side. "Our turn."

He stepped forward, and she matched his pace as they made their way to the front. Tyler wore a wide smile, anticipation and joy sparkling in his eyes as he waited for his bride.

Charlotte was a lucky woman.

When they reached the front, Adam's arm slipped from Kyla's, and she walked to stand beside Amber. Without his heat beside her, the October chill made fresh goosebumps rise on her arms. There were heaters set up around the perimeter, and slowly, they warmed her back up.

The ceremony was perfect.

To seal their marriage, Charlotte and her new husband kissed with a passion Kyla hoped to find someday. Despite her best efforts, she always seemed to end up with guys who were intelligent but boring, especially in the bedroom. Where were all the sweet, charming guys with a good sense of humor and a magical tongue?

While her dream career of caring for all creatures feathered and furry made her happy, something was missing. She wasn't looking to get married any time soon, but a boyfriend would be nice. Someone to make her laugh and go on adventures with. Someone to watch movies beside her on the couch and join her for long weekend hikes in the woods. As tempting as he was, she knew someone like Adam, who left after pulling off the condom, wouldn't fit the bill.

It would be smarter to spend her time with guys capable of more than just empty sex.

So, she'd take her cousin's advice and check out this Luke guy.

When the happy couple took off for photos and some alone time, Kyla headed into the ballroom where the reception was kicking off and stopped at the edge of the dance floor. She looked around, trying to decide whether she wanted to drink, eat, or just start dancing.

"Hey, Ky." Sandra shimmied to the Queen song blasting from the DJ booth. "Ready to party?"

"Hell yeah." Unable to resist the thudding bass, Kyla popped her hips along with the beat. "Who's Luke?"

Sandra's eyes darted left before her lips curled into a smirk like she had her own private joke. "Luke, huh?"

"Charlotte thinks we might hit it off."

"Sure. If you want him beaten half to death in the alley behind the inn."

Kyla's brows pinched. "Huh?"

Sandra laughed and leaned closer. "Adam was just walking behind you and heard you ask about Luke. If looks could kill, my bassist would be toast. Check it out for yourself."

Sandra's chin tipped up toward the opposite end of the dance floor. Adam and Zack stood at a table sipping champagne, glaring daggers at a ridiculously hot guy with dark hair and even darker eyes, chatting with a group of ladies across the room. Kyla laughed, feeling equal parts flattered and amused. And wishing she had such a sexy pool of eligible bachelors back home.

"They are pretty fucking hot." Kyla twirled the ends of her hair between her fingers as she processed the situation.

As certain as she thought she was about avoiding Adam, her stubborn, horny brain kept flitting between her options—staying in the safe zone or jumping into the deep end. She imagined herself pressed between two warm, muscled bodies, being touched, kissed, and ravaged until the sun came up. How many opportunities would she have to try something that crazy? If she passed it up, she might regret it forever.

"Did Charlotte give you the lowdown on our demented duo?" Sandra asked.

Kyla nodded. "I've been thoroughly warned. If I choose not to listen, I have only myself to blame."

"They're great guys, just not boyfriend material if that's what you're looking for. If you're looking for something else..." Sandra waggled her eyebrows. "Be safe and have fun. They're immature idiots, but they're honest and harmless. Mostly."

A woman a little taller than Sandra grabbed her by the waist and kissed her cheek.

"Kyla, this is my girlfriend, Christa. Christa, this is Charlotte's cousin, Kyla, the chick who's about to get herself into a heap of trouble."

Christa smiled. "Let me guess. Adam and Zack? I saw them checking you out a few minutes ago." Her head turned in their direction. "And again, right now."

Kyla didn't turn for confirmation, but she could *feel* their eyes on her.

"I remember how wild you were in high school," Sandra said with a laugh. "Like that time your obviously blind boyfriend called you chubby—"

"Sandra," Kyla warned.

"So you went to an amateur night at a strip club to prove he was a thickheaded moron," Sandra continued, undeterred, "and won a thousand bucks."

"Damn!" Christa's jaw dropped. "In your face, dickhead boyfriend."

It was one of Kyla's prouder moments. She'd been eighteen for only three weeks when she saw the strip club's ad in the paper. That same asshole boyfriend also told her she'd never get into vet school after one rejection letter, insisting they get a place together and work dead-end nine-to-fives instead. He'd circled a few listings in the want ads for retail, fast food, and secretarial work. *Fuck that.* The second she saw the amateur night ad, she knew she'd hit that stage and dump him afterward.

She didn't do it because she needed the outside reassurance of her hotness or an ego stroke. Or to rub it in anyone's face. Kyla wanted to make it clear to herself and that jerk that no one got to label her or put her in a box.

But hadn't she spent the last several years putting herself into one?

"Ky shook that ass like a maraca." Sandra tapped the side of Kyla's head. "If part of that girl's still kicking around in there somewhere, those boys won't know what hit them."

"Dance with me, babe," Christa said, dragging Sandra onto the dance floor by her waist. "Nice meeting you, Kyla. Have fun!"

Sandra's unexpected words poked at something inside of Kyla.

In her younger years, she embraced anything new and exciting—a spontaneous road trip to Vegas, sneaking into dive bars with a fake ID, skinny-dipping in the Willamette River.

She used to be fearless.

Then, she got into Oregon State, moved away for college, and school and work became her sole focus. Somewhere along the way, she forgot how to have a good time. She built a safe, easy life that provided routine and security but lacked color. Hell, she hadn't even taken a vacation in five years.

Refusing to give in to the temptation to glance over at Adam and Zack again, Kyla grabbed a glass of champagne off a tray and stared at the pile of gifts wrapped in silver, gold, and red paper—colors of weddings and love. If she settled down one day, would she regret all the things she didn't try and chances she didn't take?

Where did that fun, wild girl go?

As Kyla stood there surrounded by people laughing, dancing, and sipping champagne, something inside her shifted. She could feel that carefree side being slowly nudged awake by the memory of how liberating it felt to play by her own rules. To chase her bliss without shame or regret. To savor the freedom to do what she wanted, when she wanted, and who she wanted.

Speaking of which...

Tonight, she had a chance to say yes to something she once would've jumped on in a heartbeat. Some*one* she would've jumped on without talking herself out of it like she'd been doing since their paths first crossed at the pastry table.

Finally, Kyla met Adam's gaze from across the room and held it, ignoring the urge to shrink under the intimidation of his experience. Forcing herself to believe that she could handle anything he dished out. Anything *they* dished out if Zack joined in. Comfort zone, be damned.

Electric tingles of anticipation raced through her body.

That fun, fearless side of Kyla had been dormant long enough.

It was time to let her come out and play.

She smiled, a warm blush rising to her cheeks as her gaze dropped to her champagne. When she looked back at Adam, standing alone as he watched her, he mouthed something she couldn't understand.

If only she could read lips—his probably had lots of interesting stories to tell.

But even though she'd decided to jump into the deep end, those lips would have to wait. She was there to enjoy her cousin's wedding, spend time with her family, and let her hair down, not chase guys. So, Kyla spent the next few hours ignoring Adam and Zack just to make them sweat. And to see if the interest held or if they moved on to an easier or prettier target. They were players, after all, and might have their sights on several other single ladies all hopped up on the expensive champagne and romance in the air. If that were the case, she'd be disappointed, but she wouldn't let it bring her down.

Kyla made the rounds at the reception, catching up with relatives and meeting Tyler's. She ate lobster, sipped champagne, and danced her ass off. It felt good to let loose, the week's stresses melting away as the music blared and everyone celebrated the rare, beautiful love her cousin had been lucky enough to find.

There was no telling how the rest of the night would go, but no matter what, Kyla intended to have a great fucking time.

2

Adam

"**S**he knows we're watching her." Adam pulled in a breath and tossed back the rest of his champagne. "Look how hard she's trying to avoid looking over here." His head shook. "You're not fooling anyone, baby. No one's that interested in fucking wedding presents."

"She's not worth the trouble, bro." Zack grabbed a handful of Jordan almonds from the bowl at the center of the table and crunched them loudly. "Charlotte's dad keeps giving us the same death glare you were giving Luke." He popped another almond. "I gotta hit the head." He left for the bathroom, but Adam's attention never wavered.

Luke. He was fun to hang with, and the dude was talented as hell, but tonight, he was the competition. Adam wanted this girl *bad*, and he was going to fucking have her. He never felt threatened by other guys because there were plenty of ladies in the world to go around. But there was something different about this one, and he wanted to spend a few hours naked with her, trying to figure out what it was. He sure as shit wasn't going to let Luke and his bad boy haircut fuck that up.

What is it about you?

The question echoed in his mind as he watched Kyla, hoping the answer would magically come to him. She played hard to get, which he liked, but there was more to it than that.

Earlier, he'd overheard Charlotte talking about her. Kyla was twenty-five, just graduated from veterinary school, and lived alone in Corvallis. The eavesdropping alone surprised the hell out of him. Since when did he give two shits what a chick did for a living? But for some reason, the fact that her job was helping sick and wounded animals made him like her even more.

Like her?

No.

I want her. That's all it is.

But why was he relieved to hear she lived just over an hour south instead of across the country? It didn't matter where she lived when he'd only see her for a few hours and then never again. The whole thing had him confused.

Women rarely confused him. They were one half of a mutually beneficial transaction—we both get off, and then we both fuck off.

It wasn't any different when Zack was involved in the fun. And despite Zack's concerns about Charlotte's dad, Mickey, plotting their murder, he wanted her too. His best friend might take a little convincing that it was worth risking Mickey's wrath, but he'd get there. And once he did, it was game on.

Finally, Kyla gave up the avoiding eye contact game. The beautiful bridesmaid sipping champagne by the gift table met his gaze. She wore the same curve-hugging gray dress as Amber and Sandra, but hers was a few inches shorter. He'd checked out those long, toned legs several times already, and he was certain she'd caught him once or twice.

Now, she gave him a coy smile and looked down at her glass. A pretty shade of pink colored her cheeks.

Adam grinned at the delicious challenge that had just fallen into his lap.

He loved making the shy ones break out of their shell. They'd go into it blushing at the word "pussy" and end up begging for his cock. He'd have her screaming his name and begging for more by the stroke of midnight.

Sounded a lot more fun than ending the night stroking himself.

Despite her earlier rejection, he saw how her body responded to him. She wanted to give in, but something held her back. The way she looked at him now suggested maybe that resistance was weakening.

"All you have to do is say yes," he whispered.

Zack returned from the bathroom with two more glasses of champagne. "Last ones. Ty reminded me that he'll kick our asses if we get wasted tonight." A line sprung up between his brows, and he followed Adam's line of sight. "Are you fucking crazy, bro? Stop staring at that chick, and let's find one not related to the middle-aged Terminator with the scary tattoos."

Zack was right—Mickey Ross was terrifying. He was all smiles since it was his daughter's wedding day, but he looked like the kind of guy who would slit Adam's throat for even thinking about what he was thinking about. Which was how badly he'd like to slide his cock between his niece's perfect tits.

"Yup, I am fucking crazy." Adam drained his glass. "We can get around Mickey."

"She's hot as balls in July but not worth it. Even if Mickey doesn't kick your ass, Tyler will for pulling a hit it and quit it on Charlotte's cousin. Not worth the hassle. There are plenty of other choice ladies walking around. That hot blonde in the black dress was giving you serious fuck-me eyes."

Adam shook his head. "Don't care. I want *her*." Kyla had already made his dick hard twice since she arrived, and the way she licked champagne off her lips set off round three. She had the sweetest goddamn smile he'd ever seen. Plump lips that begged to be tasted. She looked shy and innocent, but there was a naughty glint in her eyes that said she just might like to be corrupted. And he wanted to be first in line to volunteer.

Zack studied his face, sighing in resignation. "I know that fucking look. I get that you like the challenge, but maybe you also have a death wish."

"Maybe."

"Stubborn shit." Zack blew out another loud breath. "Let's fucking go then."

Adam shook his head. "Not yet. I want to make her sweat. Besides, we've got toasts to give and a newly shackled brother to celebrate with."

He looked over at Tyler, smiling at Charlotte like she was his entire fucking world. Monogamy seemed like a nightmare, but they sure as shit didn't look tortured as they sucked face for the thousandth time that day. Was commitment like a wet, jiggly slab of tofu—it seems fucking disgusting until you try it made the right way?

After their toasts were given and they'd stuffed themselves on steak and cake, the sun had set. Adam was sick of waiting. Kyla was slow dancing with some guy who looked a little older and about a foot taller than she was. He was what chicks would consider handsome, and he smiled down at Kyla as his hands slid to her waist.

If this guy was imagining himself ending the night in her room, he was about to be very disappointed.

"It's go time, Zacky." Adam nudged Zack's elbow with his own. "Let's make it happen."

Kyla watched them from the corner of her eye while pretending to smile at something the dancing douche said to her. Adam wasn't fooled. The skin of her chest flushed pink, followed by her cheeks. She knew two hungry predators had her in their sights, and to her credit, she stayed right where she was and waited for the pounce.

When they reached her, the guy she was dancing with looked at them with a baffled expression that was about to be punched off his face if he didn't get his goddamn hands off her.

The song ended, and she thanked him for the dance before he scurried off, probably to find someone more in his league. This girl was a solid fucking ten, and that dickhead probably had wet dreams of someday hitting a five.

"Hey," Zack said before Adam could open his mouth. "Kayla, right?"

She opened her mouth, but before she could speak, Adam jumped in.

"No." Adam locked onto those sky-blue eyes and held steady. "It's Kyla."

Her pupils flared as she smiled that shy smile again. "Now you know my name. Happy?"

"I knew it before I asked," Adam said. "When we were getting ready, Tyler told me who I was walking with. I just wanted to see if you'd tell me."

Kyla laughed, the sound light and sweet. "And instead, I shot you down. Three times."

"She shot you down?" It was Zack's turn to laugh. "Shit, I like her already."

"Are you about to ask me to dance?" she asked, her eyes still on Adam.

"If I do, will you shoot me down again?"

She shrugged. "I guess you'll have to try it and find out."

There was something different about this interaction. *She* was different. The tension in her shoulders had released, her smile was playful and carefree. Maybe all the champagne and dancing had turned down whatever noise in her head led her to push him away earlier.

"Actually," Adam stepped closer, his fingertips itching to wipe the tiny beads of sweat from her hairline. "We came over because you're the prettiest girl here. I have a proposition for you."

Her eyebrow arched. "I bet I'm not the first girl to hear either of those lines today. You guys have quite a reputation."

"Oh, yeah?" Adam asked, intrigued. He leaned closer to be heard over the music as the next song began. "What have you heard?"

Her smile curved with a wicked edge that stirred something deep in his gut. "Enough."

Maybe he was wrong, but that smile also said their reputation wasn't a dealbreaker. Maybe even a deal*maker*.

"My cousin said I should go for Luke," she continued, "but he's a bit too..." She turned her head, and Adam followed her gaze to Luke laughing by the stage, grabbing a table to stay upright.

"Drunk?" Zack offered.

Kyla laughed. "Yeah, drunk."

Any other time, Adam and Zack would've been just as wasted. He was suddenly grateful for Tyler's lecture that made them stop after a few drinks.

A pair of muscled arms slung around Adam and Zack's shoulders from behind. Mickey Ross's dark crewcut filled the space between their heads. "I was in the Army for fifteen years, boys. Charlotte ever tell you that?"

"No, sir." Adam could count on one hand the times he'd used the word *sir* in his life, but if anyone was a *sir*, it was Charlotte's grizzled, intimidating-as-hell father, Mickey. It was easier to discount the threat he posed when his muscular arms weren't wrapped halfway around their necks.

"They taught us how to sneak up on our enemies and strike without warning." His tone was spiked with it. "Civilians have no idea how many painful and creative ways there are to kill a man. And if either of you fools lays a hand on my niece, you'll find out."

Zack's Adam's apple jumped as he swallowed. "Message received, sir."

"Don't worry, Uncle Mickey." Kyla smiled with a head tilt, her blue eyes twinkling under the house lights. "I have a boyfriend. We were just talking."

Mickey grunted, seemingly disappointed he didn't get to hunt down a shovel to dig a couple of graves. "Okay, then. You kids have fun *talking*." He squeezed their necks when he emphasized that word. He left them and walked over to chat with Tyler's mom.

"You have a boyfriend, huh?" Adam asked, disappointed but not deterred.

Kyla's smile grew. "Nope. But I didn't want to watch him tear off your arms and feed them to you."

Zack groaned, mumbling a curse. "I can already fucking tell you're a whole lot of trouble in a tiny package."

The edge of her smile rose, and her eyes glittered, the expression laced with a touch of something dirty. Adam was halfway hard again.

She licked her lips, her gaze moving south. "I can tell by the swell in your pants there's nothing tiny about *your* package." Her eyes darted to Adam's crotch, her eyebrow lifting. "All good there, too."

Adam froze.

Her words caught him off guard.

Not so shy after all.

There was nothing he liked better than a pretty girl with a filthy mouth who liked doing filthy things, but he didn't have her pegged as that.

He loved surprises, and ones this enticing were far too rare.

But... was she just fucking with them?

There had been a few women who assumed they were pigs who treated women like shit. As some sort of twisted feminist revenge, they'd play cock tease just to tell them to fuck off, leaving them to nurse their aching blue balls.

Sure, Adam and Zack didn't take women out to dinner or send flowers, but they weren't completely heartless. They just unapologetically chased pleasure and enjoyed the fruits of their stardom as any hot-blooded twenty-something male would in their position.

Kyla didn't seem like the type to play cruel games, but hopefully, she was into games of the naughty variety. She seemed to genuinely be into him, and he caught her thighs squeezing together when she first met Zack. Green lights so far.

If she wasn't down for a threesome, Zack could easily find someone else, but Adam could tell this girl would be a hell of a lot of fun to play with together. If she were brave enough to go for it, they'd make damn sure she left his room happy.

First things first. They always made their intentions clear when clothes were still on to avoid the women thinking that sharing an experience with them was something it wasn't. That seemed like a good place to start with Kyla. Adam touched her hips and moved to the music like they were dancing.

He put his lips to her ear. "Want to take the party up to my room? No rules, no strings."

Her eyes flicked across the room, and the guys turned to follow her line of sight. Mickey was scowling at them from across the dance floor.

"You're hot and all." Zack danced behind her, his mouth hovering over her shoulder. "But I'm not sure it'd be worth being chopped up and tossed in a dumpster."

The sexy sway of her hips as she danced and those plump, tempting lips had Adam convinced it would *absolutely* be worth it.

Kyla touched both of their hands, fortunately out of Mickey's line of sight. "His bark is worse than his bite, trust me. And even if he does kill you after..." She breathed against Adam's cheek, and he inhaled her sweet scent—cinnamon and vanilla, like the bear claw that started it all. "I promise you'll die a very happy man. Well, *men*."

Adam exchanged a glance with Zack. It was the one they always used when they'd just sealed the deal.

It meant *it's on.*

"You think you can handle us both?" Adam's thumb stroked her hip as he watched the steady jump of her pulse racing in her neck.

When his eyes met hers, Kyla slid her tongue along her bottom lip like she'd just eaten dessert and was savoring the last bit of cream left behind. She'd be doing the same when they were painted with his.

Adam's cock stirred again as he watched. He felt something slide up his ankle, and he looked down to find Kyla had slipped off her shoe and was stroking his skin with her toe. It was bare, just like her legs. Bare was his favorite.

Adam leaned an inch closer and caught the flare of her nostrils as she breathed him in. "Here's how it's going to go. Zack and I will say our goodbyes and head up to my suite. Five-two-six. You're going to wait twenty minutes before you join us so Uncle Mickey doesn't start sharpening his knives."

"So bossy." Her teeth clamped onto her bottom lip, drawing his eyes back to the pretty pink mouth that would look even prettier wrapped around his cock. "I like that."

"See you in twenty, princess," Zack said, his voice raspy and low. Now, he wanted her just as bad.

Game. Fucking. On.

The guys walked the room, saying goodbye to Tyler, Charlotte, and the rest of their friends. Adam's hands shook a little as he fist-bumped Tyler. If they hurt Charlotte's cousin, he'd be next in line behind Mickey to slit their dumb, horny throats.

"She's good to go, man." Zack grabbed a glass of champagne on the way to the elevator and downed it in one swallow. "Weddings get chicks so hot and bothered, we should crash them every weekend."

"Been a while since we shared." Adam hit the elevator button, and they took it to the fifth floor.

They'd fucked plenty of girls in the same room or even the same bed, and they'd shared a few dozen times, but it'd been about six months. Long overdue.

He got off on watching Zack drive a woman to scream his name while pounding her into a mattress, bathroom counter, or airplane seat. Adam was as straight as the lines on a freeway, but pleasure was pleasure. It was fucking hot watching hot people fuck.

When they got to Adam's suite, he unlocked the door, and his excitement deflated.

"Fuck." He looked at all the clothes, empty bottles, and food wrappers tossed around the bed, desk, and carpet. "Help me clean this shit up."

They did a quick sweep of the room, tossing most of the stuff in the closet and shutting it. They got out of the itchy tuxedos and took quick showers, changing into jeans and T-shirts. Adam made the bed so it wouldn't look like a mess before it was time to make another one.

"I got first dibs on her mouth," Zack said. "Did you see her lick those fucking lips of hers? I almost busted right then and there."

Adam growled with disappointment. "Fair enough. I want first crack at those tits, though."

Zack shrugged, accepting the terms.

There was a soft knock at the door, and their heads whipped toward the sound in unison.

Zack breathed into his cupped hand and slid breath spray from his pocket, spritzing a few blasts into his mouth. Adam gestured with his hand, opened his mouth, and Zack sprayed inside.

"All right, my dude." Adam fist-bumped Zack, who looked just as eager to dive in as he was. "Let's do this."

When Adam opened the door, Kyla's chin was tipped down, her long dark lashes fluttering as she looked up at him. She was so sexy and tempting, he gaped like an idiot, his gaze fixed on those beautiful blue eyes.

"Aren't you going to invite me in?" she asked. "Or are you going to fuck me right here in the hallway?"

Adam swallowed hard, opening the door and standing back to let her pass. Her shoulder grazed his chest as she walked in. He was so consumed by his craving for her that even that slight contact kicked up his pulse and made his cock spring to life.

"How much have you guys had to drink?" she asked.

"Just a few glasses of champagne," Zack answered. "We promised Tyler we'd kick back on the booze to avoid doing something stupid at his wedding. Why?"

"Because I don't fuck drunk guys. They can get rough, and not in a fun way, and sometimes they can't get or stay hard, which would be a damn waste." She slipped one strap of her dress off her shoulder. Adam bit back a groan as he stared at the newly bared skin. "For the record, I had two glasses of champagne. Which means I'll wake up with every memory of whatever happens in here and zero regrets."

Adam stepped forward, sliding off the other strap of her dress. "Then what the fuck are we waiting for?" He gripped the hair at her nape and pulled her face to his, plunging his tongue inside her mouth and swallowing her groan. After hours of craving those lips, a potent surge of desire shot through him, his cock instantly rock-hard and begging to come out and play.

She tasted like vanilla and champagne, sweet and intoxicating. Adam's eyes shut as he devoured her mouth, but he sensed Zack moving behind her. The fabric of her dress fell to the floor with a light whoosh.

"You ever have two guys at once, princess?" Zack asked. "I can already tell you're a dirty fucking girl, so I bet you have."

Adam's eyes opened to find his friend sucking and biting the skin of her shoulder and moving to her neck. Adam waited for her answer with curiosity as he unhooked her bra and brushed his lips against hers. Desperate for another taste, he plunged his tongue inside her mouth, greedily exploring every inch.

Kyla was a great fucking kisser. But skilled or not, women only got his lips at the beginning as a warm-up. Kissing felt more intimate than a blow job or slow fuck against a wall, and he didn't want them getting too attached. So, he savored it while he could. Still, he had a nagging feeling he'd be coming back for more all night long with this one.

"Not yet." She turned her head, and Zack took a turn enjoying the slide of her soft tongue while Adam dipped down to kiss the generous swell of her tits. "I'm no virgin, but you guys get to pop my threesome cherry."

Adam drew her nipple into his mouth, his tongue swirling around the beaded tip as he sucked. "I bet you taste as sweet as a fucking cherry." He slid his hand down the soft skin of her stomach and ran his knuckles along her slit, still covered in sexy black lace. "Dibs."

Zack grumbled, obviously pissed at himself for not calling it first.

"You're calling dibs on my body parts?" She chuckled low in her throat, the sound husky with need and sexy as fuck. "I'm not sure if I'm flattered or offended."

"Be flattered." Zack hooked his thumbs beneath the lace at her hips and slowly slid her panties down her legs, letting them pool on the floor with her dress. "I already called dibs on being the first to fuck that sexy mouth of yours, so I hope you'll play along."

Adam knew from his ample experience that good kissers almost always gave great head. After Zack had a go, he was definitely confirming that suspicion if she was game.

"I'll play," she breathed. Her hands threaded through Adam's hair as he grazed her other nipple with his teeth. She gasped at the jolt of pain.

"You like that, don't you, dirty girl?" Adam watched as her eyes hooded with desire before dropping to meet his.

"*Harder.*"

A hum of pleasure rumbled in Adam's throat, his cock stiffening like it was obeying her command. His teeth sank deeper, his cheeks hollowing out as he sucked until her tightening grip made his eyes water.

Zack moved beside him, feasting on the sight with a lustful, hooded gaze like the shameless voyeur he was. "Two of them and two of us." He grabbed her other breast, kneading the pale flesh before his head dipped down, taking her pebbling nipple into his mouth. Her other hand slid into Zack's hair, and she held them both to her chest as her head tipped back in bliss.

"How have I never had two mouths on me before?" Her breath came out in quick little exhales that ruffled Adam's hair. "It's so fucking intense."

Adam pulled back, releasing her breast with a soft pop. "Baby, we're just getting started." He sucked and nibbled the flesh around her nipple, leaving behind pink and purple splotches, marking her. "Before these heal, every time you look at this gorgeous body in the mirror, you'll remember how good we made you feel tonight."

It wasn't something he usually did, but for some reason, he liked the idea of haunting her for a few days with the memories of his mouth.

Adam's hand slipped over the swell of her hip and behind to grip her luscious ass. He let go and struck her cheek hard with the palm of his hand. She moaned, releasing their hair to grab the wall beside her.

"Harder," she whispered.

At that plea, Zack let out a feral growl that Adam knew all too well.

They both knew this girl was going to be a lot of fucking fun. Zack spanked her other ass cheek, and Adam hit her again, harder as requested.

Adam gripped the back of her neck and dragged her face to his, unable to resist another taste of her lips. "You like it rough, baby?" He spanked her again, harder still. Her breath caught in her throat, and before she could answer, he pressed a finger to her lips. "On second thought..." His hand slipped down her belly, his fingertips teasing the skin just above her trimmed "V" of pubic hair. "I'd rather find out for myself."

"Yes," she panted, "please."

Adam's fingers drifted lower, sliding over the soft lips of her pussy that were just as soaking wet as he knew they'd be. "Mmm..." He spanked her again, the sharp smack cutting through the charged air. His palm stung from the impact. "We hit the jackpot with this one, brother."

Adam dipped two fingertips inside her heat, sinking to the second knuckle before pulling out. Kyla's forehead fell to his shoulder, and she whimpered in his ear. As he brought his fingers to his mouth, her head lifted at the movement. She watched as he licked his fingers clean.

"I was right," Adam said, swirling his tongue around his wet fingertip. "You do taste as sweet as a fucking cherry." He slid his fingers back inside her pussy, a little deeper this time, and he offered them to Zack.

"See?" Zack grabbed Adam's wrist and sucked her juices off his fingers while his eyes stayed remained fixed to hers. "We do love to share."

Kyla's knees wobbled, and Adam pulled her to his chest. "Let's get her to the bed before she falls over. Wouldn't want her to get hurt." He smacked her ass again, and she gasped.

"I must be fucking dreaming." Her eyes went hazy, drugged with pleasure. He'd seen the look a hundred times on a hundred different faces, but somehow, it was especially beautiful on her.

Zack slipped his hands behind her head and knees, lifting her up and depositing her on the bed. "You're not, but I guaran-fucking-tee we'll be in your dreams for a while." He turned her onto her stomach, striking the cheek Adam was neglecting. Adam moved to the other side of the bed, watching as pink and then red handprints bloomed on the curve of her heart-shaped ass.

"Take off your clothes," she whispered against the pillow beneath her cheek.

"Now you're going to be the bossy one?" Adam kneeled on the bed, planting soft kisses on the handprints before sinking his teeth into her tender flesh.

Kyla's face turned and pressed into the pillow, muffling the sound of her groan.

Zack flipped her onto her back, and with her eyes trained on him, he slipped his shirt over his head and tossed it to the floor. "Get on your knees and take off my belt."

Without hesitating, she left the bed. When she was in the position on the floor, Adam knelt behind her. He swept her hair aside and covered the curve of her shoulder in wet kisses and gentle nips as her trembling fingers worked on unbuckling Zack's belt. When he got to her neck, he exhaled a hot breath in the shell of her ear, and she shivered. The heater was on in the room, so it had nothing to do with the temperature.

"Having trouble?" Adam whispered in her ear. Goosebumps rose on her arms as she fumbled with the buckle. "Let me help." He finished unbuckling the belt and slid the leather strap loose.

"Do you guys ever...?" Her eyes darted to Adam, and he grinned, knowing exactly what question was burning on her tongue.

"Ever what?" His grin widened as she stared, her cheeks flushed. He wasn't letting her off the hook. If she wanted to know something, she needed to ask.

Regardless of what she might be used to, there'd be no holding back in that room.

"Touch each other?" Kyla's throat bobbed as she swallowed. The way her pupils expanded said that the mental image in her head was one she liked. *A lot.*

Adam wasn't sure what to do with that information, but he needed to answer her question.

He slipped two fingers back inside her pussy from behind without warning, and she inhaled sharply, grabbing Zack's hips for support. "It's happened some-times, mostly by accident. Crossing swords is inevitable when you play as hard as we do." He added a third finger, and her slick inner walls clenched as they adjusted to the obviously welcome intrusion. "Pleasure is pleasure, a hand is a hand. I'm comfortable enough with my sexuality that anything that happens that feels good, I'm in."

"Speaking of pleasure," Zack said, "I can tell by the look in your eyes that you like Adam's fingers. Good work, bro."

"It's selfish." Adam's fingers dragged all the way out. He crossed them before thrusting inside with a corkscrew motion that hit her G-spot. She cried out, and her thighs squeezed his wrist, her raspy breaths growing louder, faster. "I call first dibs on this pussy, so I want it nice and wet when I slide my cock inside and make her moan."

Just thinking about finally sinking into her heat made the head of his cock swell almost painfully against his jeans. She was so goddamn tight and getting wetter with every slide of his fingers. He knew it would take every ounce of his restraint to last more than five fucking seconds inside her.

Zack cupped her chin. "I get that he's driving you wild back there, but..." His eyebrow arched. "Are you just going to let me stand here like this? Or are you going to pull down my zipper and show me what that mouth can do?"

Kyla's tongue darted out to wet her lips as she unbuttoned his fly. With trembling hands, she slipped his jeans and boxers below his hips. "Holy fuck."

Her appreciative reaction and the wetness coating her thighs said she wasn't trembling from fear. She was just as lust-drunk as they were.

"I get that a lot." Zack laughed as her eyes widened into saucers. "Wait until you see what my boy Adam's packing. I hope he's getting you nice and warmed up because you're going to need it."

Adam's fingers made a filthy wet sound as they slid in and out, fucking her fast and deep. She'd definitely be warmed up after this. "We're going to make you feel so good tonight, Kyla." He moved his slick fingers to her clit and drew wide circles that had her moaning his name. "I'm going to make you come on my fingers, then my tongue, then my cock. You said you could handle us, so we'll see if that's true."

"I can handle anything you give me." Kyla took Zack's cock into her hands and squeezed the swollen crown in her fist. Adam was a little jealous he wasn't the first one she touched like that, but since he'd be the first inside her, he couldn't complain. She glanced at Adam over her shoulder. "Spank me again. Please."

A growl rumbled in Adam's throat at her request. "So polite for such a dirty girl." Sharp smacks rang out as he painted three more red handprints onto her cream-colored flesh. "Take him into your mouth."

Zack grinned down at her. "Please."

"Mock me again, and I'll use my teeth." With a wicked grin, she bent forward and took his entire length to the back of her throat.

"I've heard chicks say he likes that." Adam chuckled. "So it's not the threat you think it is." He went back to swirling his finger over her clit, pinching the sensitive nub that he couldn't wait to tease with his tongue. His other hand slid into her hair.

"Fuck, I knew that mouth would be good." Zack's head sank back as he groaned.

Adam used his grip on her hair to get her mouth moving in the rhythm he knew Zack liked, gleaned from years of observation. "He likes long, deep strokes, just like that."

She drew her head back but kept sliding her fist over his shaft with the same rhythm. "How would you know that unless..." Her eyes blew wide, and Adam could actually feel her getting wetter around his fingers. She stayed quiet, her expression tense like she was working out a puzzle in her mind. "You said earlier that a hand is a hand, but..." She turned to Adam. "What about a mouth?"

He knew where this was going, but again, she needed to stop holding back.

"No need to be shy now, baby." Adam tightened his grip on her hair, tugging at the roots. "If there's something you want to know or want us to do to you, all you have to do it ask."

"Have you ever sucked each other's cocks?" Her voice quivered, and so did her hands as they stroked Zack from root to tip. Again, he could tell she wasn't afraid, just overtaken by the thrill of whatever she was imagining.

Zack shook his head. "Nope. I don't judge, but it's not my cup of tea. Or whisky. Whisky's better than fucking tea."

Adam kissed between her shoulder blades, working his way to her neck. "You got wetter when you asked that. Is that a fantasy you have? Watching two guys?"

Her hand stopped moving, and Zack groaned in protest. She nodded her head, but it was so slight it would've been easy to miss.

Adam kissed behind her ear, breathing more heat inside to see if he could make her shiver again. She didn't disappoint. "What's going on in that pretty little head of yours, Kyla? You want me to pop my cherry, too?" He sucked her earlobe between his teeth and nipped it before letting it go.

He wanted her to be honest, but if she said yes, could he handle that? Could Zack? It was far outside anything they'd ever done, but he decided to let her take the lead and see what happened.

Zack cupped her chin in his hand, holding her attention. "Tell us what you want."

"I want Adam..." Her throat jumped on a hard swallow. "To help me suck your cock."

Adam's eyes darted to Zack's, and their usual silent communication commenced. Adam threw him a *what do you think?* and Zack responded with a shrug that said *I'm game if you are.*

While they were often fucking random girls just for their own pleasure, some got extra special attention. If those girls had a fantasy, they loved nothing more than making it happen. Usually, that meant having two cocks in their pussy at once or being fucked in the ass and mouth at the same time. This was a new one. Adam had never touched a guy on purpose, but the idea didn't repulse him. He'd try just about anything at least once. Kneeling in front of a man didn't feel right, though, so he got to his feet.

Kyla inhaled a ragged breath as Adam sat on the bed in front of Zack. He patted the quilt beside him, and she quickly moved to the spot.

"I have a better idea," Zack said, "Take off his clothes and sit in his lap."

She gave a silent nod and undid Adam's jeans. She slipped off his shirt, and he stood, sliding his pants down his legs and kicking them away.

"You weren't kidding." Her fingertips touched her lips, shock widening her eyes. It was another look he'd seen a hundred times that looked a hundred times better on her.

Adam chuckled at her appreciative expression. "Don't worry. You'll get properly acquainted soon." He grabbed her by the waist and pulled her into his lap. His hard cock sat nestled between the cheeks of her ass, and he couldn't resist thrusting his hips a few times to enjoy the delicious friction. Kyla pressed back against him and rode his lap, the wetness of her slit coating his thighs with every teasing grind.

"I don't know whether to be excited or terrified," she said.

"Maybe both," Zack said with a snicker.

"Hey." Adam put a knuckle beneath Kyla's chin and guided her lips to his, their tongues tangling with a hunger that made the head of his cock ache for her. "No one will hurt you in this room unless you ask for it. Understand?"

She nodded. "Speaking of asking for things..."

It was easy to get distracted with her naked in his lap, but she'd made a request. One that made Adam's stomach clench with nerves, but he had no intention of backing out.

This would be... interesting.

"Show me what you want," Adam whispered against her lips.

Kyla bent forward and swirled her tongue around the head of Zack's cock. Zack hissed through his teeth before she pulled back. "I want to see you do that," she said.

A corner of Adam's mouth hitched up, and he bent forward, feeling her eyes burning into the side of his face. He gave Zack one last out with a questioning raise of his brows. The responding nod was small, but Adam heard the *okay* loud and clear.

Kyla held Zack's cock in her hand, and Adam moved closer. It was just skin, after all. If he could bend far enough, he'd be sucking his own cock five times a damn day. While Kyla watched with rapt attention, her hot breath on Adam's cheek, his tongue darted out, swiping the soft underside of the crown. Zack's throat jumped as he swallowed, his eyes trained on what Adam was doing.

No problem so far. Adam circled the head with the tip of his tongue before feeling brave and wrapping his mouth around the crown and giving it a gentle suck. There was a slight taste of salt, but the experience wasn't unpleasant.

"Fuck, dude." Zack's breathing grew shallow, his eyelids drooping. "I did not hate that."

They all laughed. Zack's laughter halted when Adam repeated the motion, going a little further down the shaft this time before pulling off. Maybe it was how comfortable he'd always been with Zack or all the crazy shit they'd done together, but it wasn't nearly as strange as he would've thought.

"That was the hottest fucking thing I've ever seen." Kyla's pussy was so drenched Adam felt her wetness slide from between her legs and onto his thighs. "Do it again. *Please.*"

Watching her get so aroused was the hottest fucking thing *he'd* ever seen. And he loved hearing her beg for more.

"Do you just like to watch?" Adam dragged his hand over Kyla's head, pushing her hair out of her eyes. "Or do you want to show me how it's done?"

Kyla's eyes shut in bliss for a second like the idea was too much to bear. He had a feeling she'd like that.

She left Adam's lap and knelt on the floor in front of Zack's left foot. Adam followed her lead and knelt on Zack's right. She leaned forward and painted one side of Zack's cock with her tongue before shooting Adam a look that made it clear she wanted him to follow her lead.

He knew right then that when they finally got to the sex, it would be absolutely goddamn mind-blowing. She was going to be so turned on that she'd be ravenous for cock, and lucky for her, they had plenty to give.

Adam licked and sucked the opposite side of Zack's shaft, and when he followed Kyla's mouth to the head, their tongues met, slipping and sliding together over the smooth, heated skin. Women had done this to them plenty of times, and it felt strange being on the giving side instead of receiving. But again, it wasn't unpleasant. Actually, it was kind of hot.

"Fuck, this is amazing." Zack stared at them in disbelief. "Why the hell haven't we done this before?"

Adam chuckled softly. "We've sure as shit done everything else at least once."

"Would you fuck him?" Kyla's question startled them both and their four eyes slipped to her face, lit up with a hopeful expression that was about to be crushed.

"Sorry, honey." Adam shook his head. "That ain't happening. But this is actually fun, so as long as I don't have to swallow anything, I'll do this as long as you want."

Zack laughed. "As usual, you read my mind, bro." He touched Kyla's cheek. "Nothing's going into this ass, and the only one I want to sink into is yours."

She sucked in a gasp. "I think I might like that." Her voice was soft and timid like she was ashamed to admit to the fantasy.

"You are a filthy fucking girl, aren't you?" Adam grabbed her nape and kissed her hard, Zack's cock standing at attention below their faces. Adam was impressed by how bold she was growing in asking for what she wanted. She definitely deserved a reward. "Why don't we show Zack how wet you are from helping me suck him off?"

"Fuck, yes." Zack wrapped his hand around his cock, watching as Adam took her hand and sat on the bed, tugging her back into his lap.

He touched Kyla's knees and pulled them apart, hitching the backs over the tops of his thighs. She whimpered as he slipped a hand between her legs and spread the silky lips wide. "Look at that pretty pink pussy. All nice and wet for us. Ready to stretch and be filled."

"*Please*." Her head fell back onto his shoulder. "You're killing me here."

Zack hummed in his chest as he stroked himself. "Make her come, Adam. She's fucking earned it."

"I agree." He dragged the backs of his knuckles up the side of her neck as she panted in his ear. "And since you're getting so good at telling us what you want, you get to choose. Do you want my fingers?"

Adam plunged three fingers inside, finding her G-spot and rubbing with a beckoning motion that made her jump an inch off his lap with a buck of her hips.

"*Fuuck*." Her nails bit into the side of his knee.

Adam wrapped an arm around her waist, and she settled again, accepting the pleasure he gave. "Or do you want my mouth?"

Adam pulled his fingers from her, and she exhaled through her nose with obvious frustration. She watched as his hand rose to his lips, and he slowly licked the length of his glistening finger. Zack grabbed his wrist and sucked the remaining two fingers at once. Adam was caught off guard when the sensation made his cock jump against her back.

"He liked that," Kyla whispered, her tone dark and naughty. "I want your mouth, but first… I think it's Zack's turn to pop his cherry."

Zack's lips scrunched and moved to the side like he was thinking. He was never one to back down from a challenge or an opportunity to try something new in the bedroom, but this was beyond anything either of them had done before.

"You don't have to—" Adam's words died when Zack sank to his knees in front of them.

Adam and Kyla stilled as Zack inched closer, buried the head of Adam's cock between his lips, and sucked. Adam gripped the blankets beneath him in his fists at the rush of sensation.

The realization that Zack had tasted him before the girl in the room left him dumbstruck. This was brand new territory, and he hoped like fuck it wouldn't change anything in their friendship. None of the other crazy shit they'd done ever had. And it's not like this would be a regular thing. It was fulfilling a fantasy for a white-hot chick who'd asked so nicely with her long eyelashes fluttering as if any part of her was innocent.

He gripped the base of Adam's cock and stroked, the head disappearing again inside the warm, wet "O" of his lips. After one more pass, he pulled off with a wet pop. "Your turn, princess."

Adam gripped the blankets harder in anticipation.

Zack held Adam's shaft while Kyla got to her knees on the carpet beside him. Her lips parted, and as her warm, wet mouth slid over Adam's length, a loud groan rose from his throat. Their eyes locked, and the sight of her swallowing his cock made his balls clench. She worked him with her mouth while Zack's fist squeezed around the base, jerking Adam closer and closer to the edge.

"I'm almost there," Adam breathed, lost to the pleasure. "If you don't want to swallow, you better pull back now."

Zack grinned. "Lucky for you, Kyla, my boy can go three or four times in a night. Like a fucking machine."

Her mouth popped off, and she held Adam's gaze. "I want to taste you."

Fucking hell. The feeling was mutual.

"You didn't say please." Adam's lip curled at her glare of faux impatience.

"Pretty please with sugar on top," she said. "Come in my fucking mouth."

Zack grabbed a fistful of her hair and guided her back to Adam's cock. Once she found the rhythm that made his hips twitch and his breaths quicken, she held steady. He was right back on the edge in seconds, his balls tight and aching with the need for release.

"Suck him deeper, princess." Zack let go so she could take him all the way to the back of her throat. Once Adam's entire cock disappeared between her lips, she sucked hard and swallowed around the head. "That's it."

"Fuck!" Adam's body tensed, and his hips thrust upward to meet her mouth. Finally, he burst onto her tongue, flooding her throat with his climax as her pace slowed. Her lips sealed around the head until there was nothing left, and when she let go, he was coated in sweat, struggling to catch his breath. "You're fucking incredible, Kyla."

She sat back on her heels and swallowed hard, wiping the corners of her mouth that curled up in a satisfied grin. "That was fun." There was a glistening dot left on her bottom lip, and he gathered it with his thumb and pushed inside. She sucked it clean.

She'd made Adam come so hard his goddamn toes tingled.

And he was eager to return the favor.

Without a word, he threw Kyla over his shoulder and tossed her back onto the bed while she laughed.

"I'll show you fun, sweetheart." He got to his knees and spread her long legs wide before settling between them. After taking a moment to enjoy the view, he used his thumbs to stretch her lips, opening her up before plunging his tongue inside her dripping hole.

Zack sat on the edge of the bed beside her pillow, his fist wrapping around his cock while he watched them. "I've seen that tongue make pretty girls like you cry." He chuckled darkly as he stroked himself. "But only when he stops."

"I don't fucking doubt it." Kyla reached for Adam's shoulders, her fingernails biting into his skin.

Adam lapped at her slit with long, languid strokes before focusing on the hood around her clit. He drew the silky skin between his lips and gave a quick flick to the tiny nub, testing to see what she liked. Eating pussy was one of his favorite hobbies, and Kyla's was one of the prettiest he'd seen. And she tasted like fucking heaven. He could feast between her legs until the sun came up, and even then, he'd dive back for more.

Zack's fingertips grazed the pink and purple marks Adam had left behind on her breast. "It's not fair if only he gets to mark you." His head dipped to her chest, and he licked the top of her right breast before sucking the flesh into his mouth. Her nails scraped down his back as he repeated the motion until she was decorated with five new marks.

"I sure as fuck don't need hickeys to remember you two." Her eyes squeezed shut, and she cried out at what Adam was doing with his tongue.

He slipped two fingers inside and put his free hand low on her stomach, pressing down to grant better access to her G-spot. When he hit it just right,

Kyla groaned before mumbling a string of curses that made him grin. They'd learned a trick or two over the years and probably knew more about the female anatomy than some gynecologists.

"Although," she continued, "I do appreciate feeling claimed."

The word sizzled in Adam's gut. He sealed his mouth over her mound and sucked until she cried out again.

Were they *claiming* her?

Did she want them to? Or was this part of the fantasy? Hell, he wasn't even sure what the word meant to her, and he was too busy savoring her pussy to give it much thought. He slipped his tongue inside her again and groaned from a wave of pleasure when her juices dripped to his chin. Her belly tensed beneath his hand, and her hips bucked. She was close.

"You going to come in my mouth, baby?" Adam asked with a teasing flick of his tongue. "I want to feel this pussy grip my tongue when you let go."

"I'm..." she panted, "close."

"Kiss those pretty pink lips, Zack." Adam ran a thumb along her bottom lip. "While I keep kissing these."

Kyla's breath caught in her throat as Adam held her hips to the bed and attacked her clit with the tip of his tongue. "It's too much. I can't—"

"Yes, you can." Zack kissed her hard, sucking her bottom lip as he pulled back. "Take everything he gives you. Don't fight it."

Adam held her down as she wiggled to break free of his hold, but she didn't say no or tell him to stop—not exactly. So she was going to damn well surrender to him and the relentless assault of his mouth.

"Oh, fuck, oh, fuck..." She kept chanting it like a prayer, but no god could save her now. Finally, a rumbling, primal growl cracked in her chest, and she grabbed Adam's hair in both fists as she came. She used the hold to press him to her center, his tongue never letting up. She humped his face, and he growled in approval, sliding his hands beneath her ass to hold her even closer. She coated his nose, lips, chin, and thank whatever god she prayed to, his tongue. He hoped her taste stayed branded there for the rest of his life.

Wait.

What?

Kyla's arms flopped to the bed like they were boneless, and she was quiet while she caught her breath. "No one has ever…"

Adam cocked a cocky eyebrow. "Ever what?" And thankfully, they still had a very cock-y night ahead of them.

"Made me come that way." She exhaled loudly, her arm drifting up to cover her eyes. "I was starting to think it wasn't possible."

"Another cherry popped?" Zack asked. "This *is* a special fucking night."

Adam crawled up her body, his weight pressing her against the mattress as he kissed her. "Special is right. There's something different about this one, eh, Zacky?"

Usually, the word "special" made him want to puke, but in her case, it fucking fit.

3

Kyla

They thought she was *special*?

Kyla was shocked that the word was even in their vocabulary. It was impossible not to wonder if they said to all the women they'd been with, but since they wanted them to leave and never look back, it was doubtful. Why bother trying to flatter someone you'll never see again?

"Talking about me like I'm not even here?" Her gaze narrowed, but her lips twitched with the smile she held back. "That's rude, and I'm severely offended. You'll have to make it up to me somehow."

"After you drink water," Adam said, "and I get rid of some."

"Gross." Kyla wrinkled her nose as he grabbed a water bottle from the mini fridge and handed it to her. She sat up cross-legged at the center of the bed.

She chugged the whole thing in a few deep swallows, and when Adam finished up in the bathroom, he flopped onto his back beside her. His sexy tattoos were distracting, so she moved onto her belly, tracing them with her fingertip.

A trail of musical notes ran from his right shoulder to the center of his chest. The letters "T" and "M" were at the center of a swirling design that she guessed was their band logo. The word *loyalty* was etched on his bicep, and she noticed earlier that Zack had the same one. She admired their bond, and it made her miss her friends back home in Portland.

"So, what's the story, princess?" Zack lay on his back on the opposite side of the bed with his hands tucked behind his head, getting comfortable. Earlier,

Kyla had worried about feeling intimidated around them, but she was strangely comfortable, too. "Why no boyfriend? The dudes in Corvallis don't know how to eat a pussy or what?"

Kyla laughed. "In my experience, they don't. I go on dates now and then, but I always end up bored before the entrees arrive." She poked his ribs above the tattoo of a black lightning bolt. His ink was distracting, too. "Not everyone's a sexy rockstar full of fun, dirty stories to tell."

"Shame," Zack said. "Because it's pretty fucking rad."

"I bet." She huffed a laugh, wondering why Adam was being so quiet all of a sudden. "You've never met a girl who made you want more than this?"

Then, Zack went quiet.

Adam looked over and frowned, his expression filled with obvious concern for his friend. "Zack, you don't have to—"

"Once. Didn't work out."

Kyla scooted closer to Zack, folding her hands beneath her chin as they rested on his stomach. "She must've been really special to convince you to try."

He scoffed, his body going rigid. "Fucking understatement. She was perfect."

Kyla planted a soft kiss on his ribcage, offering the comfort she could sense he needed. He sighed, his tense muscles relaxing into the bed. "What happened?"

Zack shrugged. "Couldn't handle what my life is. I was never around, and she needed more. She fucking deserves more."

"So do you," Kyla said.

She meant it. Even though she didn't know them well, she could tell they both accepted less than they deserved. As much as they clearly loved women and sex, it must be deeply lonely to not feel safe enough to let people in. And in Zack's case, to have it sour when you finally try.

"Call her, Zack," she said. "Maybe her circumstances have changed. Or maybe she's been thinking about you all this time, hoping you'll reach out. You might regret it if you don't."

Zack met Kyla's gaze, the sadness in his eyes making her throat tight. "Maybe." Finally, he looked away, fiddling with the chain around his neck. "Someday."

"You guys are being huge fucking bummers." Adam sat up and handed Kyla a controller for the Sega Genesis console hooked up to the big-screen TV before grabbing another for himself. "Let's get a few rounds of fighting in before a few rounds of fucking, yeah?"

"Sure." She held back a smile when the screen came on, and she saw what game it was. *Mortal Kombat 3.* This was going to be fun. "Is it easy to play?"

"Just try out the buttons," Adam said. "I'll go easy on you until you figure out what they do."

"Thanks." She scooted to the end of the bed, facing the screen. Zack and Adam moved to either side of her.

Once they picked their characters and the announcer gave the order to fight, Kyla had Adam's character in a bloody pool on the ground in ten seconds flat.

"What the fucking fuck?" He gave her a sidelong glance and sat up straighter the next round, determination in his eyes.

"Hell yeah, Kyla!" Zack busted up laughing, light returning to his expression. "She fucking dusted you, dude!"

She grinned, her shoulders lifting in a shrug. "Beginner's luck."

When the next round kicked off, Adam's fingers flew over the buttons, but it was hopeless. In seconds, his character was toast while Zack doubled over in hysterics. As round three began, Adam squared his shoulders, his knuckles white as they gripped the controller. She almost felt guilty for what she was about to do.

"Did you just turn me into a goddamn *baby*?" Adam's jaw hinged open while his eyes bulged—a look she'd seen before.

Guys weren't used to women kicking their ass at video games, which made doing it even more satisfying.

"You've never heard of a babality?" Kyla chuckled. "Amateur."

In college, she blew off steam after classes in a club with other female gamers. While most of her peers were getting wasted at frat parties, she was learning how to do this.

Adam's character was bleeding and headless at her character's feet.

"I've never been more turned on in my entire goddamn life." Zack gaped at the screen.

"Weird kink you got there, Zack." Kyla bumped his shoulder.

Adam was breathing loudly beside her, as if he'd just sprinted from the other end of the room. She won two more rounds before yanking out his character's spinal cord with another brutal fatality.

Adam's controller slipped from his fingers and hit the floor. He turned to her.

She stared in confusion until his lips were crashing into hers. He pressed her into the mattress with his body and seized her wrists, pinning them over her head.

"I guess you guys have the same kink." Kyla caught her breath and kissed him again. She loved giving up control to these men who knew exactly how to use it to drive her fucking crazy. As the kiss grew deeper, more urgent, she sank further into the bed, surrendering to his hold.

Adam broke the kiss. "Got any other hidden talents, sweetheart?" His teeth sank into her neck, and he sucked the skin hard before pulling back, his eyes searching hers.

"Maybe." She arched a brow. "But since you'll be kicking me out soon, I guess you'll never find out."

Adam's eyes narrowed, but he didn't look away. She swore there was something different about how he looked at her compared to earlier in the night. The predatory hunger aimed her way at the reception was still there, but now, it was layered beneath something less shallow. It would be useless to give it much thought since the night would be over soon, but still, it was... interesting.

"Guess not," he said with a tone that seemed edged with disappointment, adding to her confusion. Of course, maybe she was imagining it, and nothing had changed for him at all.

"Ready for more?" Zack's hand ghosted up her ribcage, and she shivered.

Kyla tore her gaze from Adam. "Hell yes."

Adam crawled backward, and when he reached her ankles, he turned her onto her stomach. "Hips up." He reached under her waist and pulled her middle upward. "Put that gorgeous ass in the air for me."

He stood at the foot of the bed, and Zack joined him.

Adam rubbed his rough palm along the curve of her bottom. "Isn't that a fucking sight?" His hand stilled over her cheek, which was tender and probably red from earlier. Kyla panted with anticipation. He knew damn well what she wanted, and she sensed he was going to make her work for it. "You like a dash of pain with your pleasure, don't you, baby?"

She nodded against the quilt.

"Is there anything else you want to ask for?" Zack mimicked Adam's movement, his hand settling on the opposite cheek. "How far do you want to go?"

Adam struck first, and Zack followed. Her moan was muffled by the quilt beneath her.

"Don't you dare." Zack pinched her chin and forced her head to the side, her cheek resting against the fabric. "We want to hear you. Every moan, whimper, and scream we wrench out of this soft, sexy body."

"I want you to fuck me," she said, answering his question. "Hard."

"I claimed your pussy first." Adam bent forward and swiped his tongue over her dripping slit from behind. Her inner walls clenched in response, begging for more than his tongue. "Is that okay with you, sweetheart?"

Kyla nodded against the bed, unable to speak or think or move.

Adam fisted her hair and yanked her to her knees, stealing the air from her lungs. His lips tickled the shell of her ear, and she shivered, goosebumps rising on her skin. "I need you to say it. Fuck me, Adam. Fuck my cunt so hard every time I try to sit down tomorrow, it'll hurt." He nipped her earlobe, and she gasped. "And I get the feeling you'll fucking love that burning sting."

He released her hair and gripped her throat with his freed hand. A small burst of panic kicked up her pulse, but it quickly turned to lust. She struggled to swallow beneath his hold.

"Fuck me, Adam." Kyla groaned as his hand squeezed tighter, fire racing through her blood. "I want it hard, and I fucking want it *now.*"

Her demanding tone made him chuckle, low and ominous like the rumble of thunder. Another shiver crawled up her spine.

Adam released her throat. "You're about to get exactly what you asked for by coming into a hotel room with two men who live for this shit."

By his tone, Kyla knew it was both a warning and a promise.

And she couldn't wait to get what was coming to her.

Adam snatched his jeans off the floor and pulled a handful of condoms from his back pocket. "This is all I've got." He tossed them onto the bed and jerked his chin at Zack. "Let's make them count."

Five square packets lay scattered across the quilt.

Adam grabbed one, tearing it open with his teeth before slipping it over his length and pinching air out of the tip. Kyla was relieved they'd come prepared. She'd never had an STD or a pregnancy scare, and she sure as shit wasn't starting tonight, no matter how much she'd love to feel them sink inside her, bare and raw.

"Hold up." Zack slid underneath her, face to face. "I want to taste these lips while you moan and squirm." He kissed her while Adam knelt behind her on the bed, grabbing one of her hips.

Without being able to see what he was doing, she felt vulnerable but not scared. It was heady to anticipate his next touch and where it would land. His body heat told her when he moved closer to her center, and she imagined him lining himself up to surge forward without warning. Her fists clenched in the blankets, waiting.

"Your pussy is creaming for me, Kyla." Adam slid a finger over her wetness, and she whimpered at the teasing touch. "If it hurts, tell me to stop."

She had enough experience to know she could handle big. Adam put those other guys to shame, but women's bodies were built to stretch and adjust. Desire surged through her core as he positioned the tip of his cock at her entrance and stopped, seemingly waiting for her confirmation. Obviously, they were fine with inflicting a little pain, but she knew he didn't want to injure her. So, he was trustworthy with her lady bits, after all.

"I understand," she said over her shoulder. "Fuck me, *please*."

Adam pushed his hips forward, sinking into her slowly, stopping when the tip breached her entrance. She tried pushing back against him, but he grabbed her hips, holding onto the control.

"Easy at first, baby." His thumbs brushed against her hips, soothing her as she shuddered with want. "When I know you can take me, I'll pound this pussy until tears fall down those soft pink cheeks."

He spanked her without warning, and she let out a groan that was stifled by Zack's eager mouth. She couldn't believe how turned on she was, her inhibitions falling further every second, allowing her to fully enjoy both of them. It didn't matter that the world outside that door would judge her and them for what they were doing. All that mattered was pleasure and sensation, giving and receiving so everyone would leave happy. What was so wrong with that?

Adam slipped in another inch, and Kyla felt her inner muscles stretch, adjusting to his size. Another inch had her clawing at the headboard.

"Doing okay?" Adam stopped, waiting.

"Fuck yes," she panted. "*More.* I can take it."

As he sank in a little deeper, her G-spot came to life, helping to loosen the tight grip of her pussy to let him in a little further. Had she ever been this fucking wet? She'd probably be embarrassed with anyone else, but she could tell they loved it. The way they appreciated seeing her experience pleasure proved that the rumors they were purely selfish in the bedroom were nonsense.

Adam stopped again when he was at least halfway home. Zack gave him a thumbs-up beside her shoulder.

"What was that for?" she asked.

"I'm good at telling when a girl's struggling to adjust," Zack explained. "That's why we get started in a position where I can see your face if Adam can't."

"So, a thumbs-up—" The air left her lungs as Adam sank deeper, deeper, until he was seated all the way. His balls bumped her pussy, and she moaned deep and low at the heady sensation of being thoroughly, deliciously filled. Her wrists gave out, and she leaned against Zack's chest for support.

"Means you can take him all the way," Zack said with a knowing grin. "I was right because that didn't sound painful at all. That was the sound of pure fucking bliss."

"It was a beautiful sound." Adam slid out to the tip and surged back inside her in one push. "I wonder if I can get her to make it again."

She was so wet, she knew his balls were coated as they slapped against her clit with noises that were filthy and primal and hot as all hell.

"You're so fucking tight, Kyla." Adam withdrew and thrust his hips forward. "Your mouth was amazing, but this pussy is fucking heaven. Still doing okay?"

Okay didn't cover it. How the hell did she go so long without getting good and fucked, relying on silicone toys to get her off that could never feel as good as this. She'd missed kissing nearly as much and wanted more of that, too. Zack was good, but the way Adam devoured her mouth was positively addictive. Knowing their time was short, she wanted to feel it again while he was inside her.

Kyla glanced over her shoulder. "Flip me over and see for yourself."

His mouth tilted in a crooked grin as he pulled out and did as he was told, flipping her onto her back beside Zack. Her breasts shook with the movement, and Adam dipped his head, giving her one more mark to remember him by right above her left nipple. Kyla enjoyed a little pain with sex and was grateful they hadn't gone too far. Maybe their experience taught them what limits to stick to on a first date. Of course, they never had a second, so maybe that was as far as they ever went.

Zack slid to the edge of the bed, his cock in his hand. "I'm just going to watch for a while. You guys look fucking hot together."

Kyla didn't love the phrasing—they weren't *together*, but she knew what he meant. Two bare bodies merging and moving together was a sexy sight.

Adam hovered over her, their lips brushing while his cock nudged at her opening. Their eyes connected, and heat tingled in her throat. He was so close, his breath ruffled the hair at her temples, and she could see the flecks of hazel in his irises. Three tiny freckles dotted the skin of his left cheek in the shape of a triangle.

"You're really fucking beautiful, Kyla." Adam's eyes never wavered as he slid back inside and kissed her gently.

It felt strange to be scrutinized by someone who'd probably slept with models and actresses, but he didn't look at her with anything but appreciation. The soft smile on his lips made him seem more real somehow. Like the tough, playboy façade slipped for a moment, and she glimpsed a man who was capable of more than he gave himself credit for. It was hard to look away.

It was then that Kyla realized, despite her best judgment, that she liked Adam. A small line popped between his eyebrows like he was suddenly just as baffled as she was by what was happening between them.

Did he feel that too?

Their gaze held as he bucked his hips and sank deeper. Kyla's eyes fluttered closed. She used the broken connection to catch her breath after whatever the hell that was.

Adam picked up his pace, his hips slamming against hers. She'd asked for it hard, so she was getting it hard. Every time their eyes met, she got that same tingling feeling, but it was spreading lower, settling in her chest.

It was too much. When they finished, she would put some space between them so lines wouldn't be blurred. For either of them. As if he'd read her mind, he tore his gaze from her, burying his face in the curve of her neck.

No.

That's not what she wanted either. To feel like just another faceless hole.

Her lips grazed his ear as she whispered, "Look at me, Adam."

There was a brief stutter in the rhythm of his thrusts before the steady pace returned. Adam buried his face deeper into her neck like he was pretending he hadn't heard her. Maybe the strange feeling had thrown them both off. Although everything below her waist felt incredible, everything above her shoulders was suddenly confused as hell.

"Don't hide." Kyla cupped the sides of his face in her hands and forced him to obey. "Look me in the eyes when you're inside me so I don't feel like I'm just another body to you."

Adam shook his head as their gaze held, his heavy exhales warm on her skin. "Impossible."

"What are you two whispering about?" Zack asked, still stroking his cock while he watched.

"Nothing," they said in unison. Then, they smiled in unison.

Maybe she wasn't just another body to him. She wasn't expecting poems and flowers, but she deserved to have his mind and all the rest of him while she was with them.

Adam slowed his movements, and her legs wrapped around his hips, her ankles hooking together. "You feel so fucking good, Kyla."

He kissed her eyelids and cheeks before angling his face and capturing her lips. His tongue explored her mouth, and she moaned as he fucked her harder, deeper. The scruff of his beard was rough against her skin, but it only added to the layers of sensations overwhelming her senses.

"So do you," she said. "Don't stop."

Adam shifted his hips, instantly hitting her G-spot like he had a damn map. Kyla moaned again, the sound deep, desperate, and so loud she'd be embarrassed if she wasn't so lost in the pleasure. She had trouble finding the spot herself sometimes, and few men she'd been with had even bothered to try.

"Hey, Zack, we could use a hand." Adam propped himself up on his wrists. "Rub her clit until she comes."

"Happy to help." Zack stuck his fingers in his mouth, wetting them.

"Open your legs for him, baby." Adam tapped her hip, and she released his waist, setting her feet on the mattress and spreading them wide.

Zack's hand slipped between their bodies, and when he found her clit, warm sparks of pleasure spread through her core. It was almost too much, and she clawed at the bedspread beneath her. All those hours playing bass had obviously made those fingers incredibly strong and good at hitting their mark.

"I think you found the spot." Adam chuckled, watching her expression from above as she focused, chasing her pleasure. "Tell him what you need, Kyla."

"Press harder," she said in a rough, raspy voice that sounded foreign to her ears. "And tighter circles."

Zack's hand shifted between them, and when he got it right, her pussy squeezed Adam's cock and a surge of wetness slickened his movements.

"That's it," Adam said. "Good job, bro. I bet Kyla's going to thank you for that when I'm done with her."

Kyla felt the wounded look sweep across her features before it vanished as quickly as it came. Even though she knew he didn't mean that the way it sounded, his words stung. But that was the reality of the situation. Soon, they would both be done with her, and she'd scurry off, as agreed. She was a big girl, so she'd accept it and move on with her life. At least she'd be left with plenty of sweet, filthy memories to replay in her mind for years to come.

Despite the growing, incredibly inconvenient desire she felt for something more with Adam, that would have to be enough.

4

Adam

As Adam took Kyla hard and deep, alongside the pleasure was confusion. Since that first scorching look she'd given him after the pastry swap in the lobby, he sensed something was special about this girl. He still couldn't put his finger on exactly what it was, but the answer felt closer than ever.

Sure, there were obvious differences between her and his usual hook-ups that put points in her corner. Kyla didn't come up to his room because he was famous or had more money than sense. She wasn't interested in boosting her career by standing beside him in photos or sitting beside him at awards shows. She was there to have a good time and from the looks of it… mission fucking accomplished. But there was more to it. Something about her was inexplicably drawing him in.

Regardless of whether or not he solved the mystery, the goodbyes would come soon. But instead of the chick crying and begging to see him again, Adam was going to be the problem. Because he knew damn well he wouldn't be done with Kyla after one night.

And he had absolutely no clue what to do with that.

"Fuck, Adam," she breathed, "I'm going to come." Their gaze held as her eyelids sank low. He really liked the sound of his name on her lips. He didn't know what to do with that either. "Come with me."

In a night of cherries popping like mad, that would be another if it could be done. Usually, the girl got off, and then he did. Sharing an intense experience blurred lines.

Hell, what did he have to lose by trying one more crazy fucking thing?

Adam sped up his movements, chasing the orgasm that was right within reach. A few short, quick thrusts tugged him closer, and as her pupils flared and her legs squeezed around him, he came with a groan in the soft, sweet-smelling curve of her neck. His arms wrapped around her and held her close as her climax took her to the same beautiful place.

Kyla's arms circled his back, and she planted a line of gentle kisses on his neck, shoulder, and finally, on a sensitive spot behind his ear. "You. Are. Incredible."

She whispered it for only him to hear, and he felt a pang of guilt. He never wanted Zack to feel like a third wheel, but how was that possible?

What in the ever-loving fuck is going on?

Zack laughed. "Can I have my hand back?"

Adam moved off of her and stood to free Zack's trapped hand and to put some distance between him and Kyla so he could get his head on straight. He went into the bathroom, pulled off the condom, tossed it into the toilet, and flushed.

It was undeniable that something had shifted between him and Kyla. Like some of the carefree playfulness from earlier in the night had been replaced with something a lot more complicated. He had nothing to offer a woman like her, and it was unfair to let her think otherwise. After splashing cold water on his face, he knew what had to be done.

The kissing had to stop. Staring into her pretty blue eyes had to go too. Things needed to stay purely physical, or it all had to end.

He was hoping to find a turn-off that would make it easier to keep her at a distance. Maybe she trimmed her toenails with her teeth or chewed with her mouth open. Or chewed her toenails with her mouth open. A guy could only hope.

Adam walked to the mini fridge, poking around inside. "Anyone else need a fucking gallon of water?" He pulled out two small bottles and handed them to

Zack and Kyla. "The tap water here smells like a fish tank, so this is the best we got."

He felt Kyla's eyes on him as he grabbed another bottle and brought it to his lips, gulping it down in three deep swallows.

"That was one hell of a show." Zack chugged his water and wiped his mouth with his wrist. "Still up for more?"

Kyla shot Adam a sidelong glance before nodding. "Absolutely. You didn't get to come yet, and there are still four condoms left. I'm up for the challenge if you guys are."

Adam tilted his head to the side, studying her. With her confident smile and the naughty sparkle in her eyes that drew him in on the dance floor, she did seem ready for more. Hopefully that didn't change when he redrew the boundaries that had somehow been crossed.

"Do you guys have any snacks up here," Kyla asked, "or just booze?"

"I'll order room service," Adam said, grabbing the phone. He appreciated the task because it let him focus on something other than worrying about hurting her. "What do you want?"

She tapped her lips. If Kyla was like most of the girls he'd hooked up with when it came to food, she was probably thinking about which salad dressing had the fewest calories. "Fries," she said, "and a side of ranch."

Damn. He should've known she'd be different with that, too. After all, she had a pastry for breakfast instead of black coffee and air like the salad addicts. She obviously took care of herself but he liked that she ate real food and had curves he could grab onto.

"Get me a cheeseburger," Zack said. Only he would chase the steak and lobster they'd eaten just a couple of hours ago with a damn burger. "And a beer."

Adam placed the order along with a beer and fries for himself. They sounded good as soon as she'd said it. Kyla was full of great ideas that night, and he couldn't wait to hear the next one. Hopefully, it involved his mouth between her legs again.

On the way back to the bed, Adam's big toe slammed into the metal bed frame. "Fucking bloody hell!" A red-hot burst of pain shot up through his leg and radiated through his foot. He hopped to sit on the edge of the bed, inspecting the wound as red seeped through a half-inch gash in his skin.

"Are you okay?" Kyla knelt on the floor in front of him. "Let me see."

He reflexively jerked his foot back when she reached for it. "I've got it."

The corners of her mouth tipped down in an impatient frown. "You split your nail, and you're bleeding, Adam. I'm a medical professional. Give me your goddamn foot."

"I'm not a Pomeranian," he snapped. Regret heated his face as the pain throbbed in his toe. He'd been taking care of himself since he was sixteen and didn't like people fussing over him. His parents were great, but when they divorced, they were too busy trying to make the other one's life miserable to pay him much attention. He was used to paying his own bills, cleaning up his own messes, and putting on his own damn bandages.

"No, but you're being kind of an asshole," Zack said, leaning over to see the damage. "Let her check it out. She's a fucking doctor."

Adam huffed, raising his hands so she could get a closer look.

Kyla supported his heel with one hand and gently touched the sides of his toe to hold it still as she inspected the wound. "Be right back." She got a few things from the bathroom before digging through her purse and pulling out a few supplies.

"I'll just rinse it off," Adam protested, "and wrap it in toilet paper until the bleeding stops."

"No," she said, "you won't. That's how you get an infection."

Zack laughed. "Never thought I'd see the day when Adam Fucking Hyatt was pussy-whipped."

Adam kicked him in the shin with his uninjured foot.

Kyla knelt back on the floor and dabbed at the blood with a damp tissue that smelled like soap. "The bleeding's almost stopped, but the split nail's going to hurt for a few days."

She opened a bandage and put a dot of ointment on the pad before carefully placing it over the wound and securing the adhesive strips. Her hair fell over her eyes as she worked, and Adam tucked it behind her ear, earning him a smile as gentle and sweet as her touch. Women were never sweet with him. They sure as hell never went out of their way to take care of him like this. Even his own mom would've stuck the toe under the bathtub faucet and called it a day.

He hadn't even realized this was something he wanted until that moment.

"Thanks." Adam assessed her work. An orange and black Garfield bandage covered the entire injury, and the throbbing had stopped—much more effective than a wad of toilet paper would've been. It was also fucking adorable that she carried cartoon bandages in her purse. "And I'm sorry."

"You're welcome." Kyla bent forward, holding his gaze as she pressed a kiss over the bandage. The unexpected gesture made his heart thump like a kick drum. Why did she have to be so fucking perfect? "At least you didn't try to bite me. A Pomeranian would've."

He was an asshole for saying that. The pain, combined with his twisted-up head, made him lash out. It was no excuse, but obviously, she didn't hold it against him.

It was one of the countless reasons why Kyla Ross was too good for him. That fact was undeniable, but the connection between them was undeniable, too. Still, she deserved more than Adam could offer, so the boundaries needed to be clearer for everyone in the room. It was a shame the last kiss he'd accept for the night was on his damn foot, but it had to be that way. Things needed to go back to being playful and casual. No strings, as promised.

"We all know you would've liked it." Adam took Kyla's hand and nipped the tip of her finger while she laughed.

"I would've bitten you back," she said, seizing his wrist. Her smile grew as she sank her teeth into his forearm.

The corners of his mouth tipped up. This girl was a lot of fucking fun, and her sunshine-and-lollipops energy was infectious. Still, he had to pull back. He didn't want to watch the joy in her expression collapse if he turned cold without warning, so he'd pull a different play from his trusty detachment handbook to pair with the "no more kissing." Few things were more unsexy in his world than a poseur, so that was where he'd aim.

"Women think I'm tasty," Adam said, "but they're always tryin' to waste me."

She'd worn a Rolling Stones shirt before the wedding. Did she buy it because she thought the lips and tongue on the logo were cute? Or was she one of those people who bought a band's merch because one song on the radio made them smile? It would be a guaranteed boner-killer if she was.

Her eyebrow lifted. "And make me burn the candle right down," she sang, her perfect pitch and husky voice shooting straight to his cock.

Holy fuckin hell.

"Tumbling Dice" wasn't a radio song. And it was on *Exile on Main Street*—not only the best Stones album but one of the best rock albums of all time. Adam's attempt at disliking her had exploded right in his face, backfiring like a rusted old Chevy. Now, he wanted to hear her sing again. He wanted to ask about her favorite bands and a thousand other questions he'd never cared enough to ask someone who'd been naked in his bed.

"Any more special requests, special girl?" Zack planted a kiss on her shoulder and hooked his hand around her waist.

Zack's question shook Adam from his thoughts and had him ready for another round.

"I want Adam in my mouth while you fuck me."

How did he ever think this girl was shy?

"A classic," Zack said with a grin. "And one of our favorites. You must've really liked having him come inside that pretty mouth." Zack moved in front of her, tipping her chin back to kiss up the column of her throat.

Kyla grabbed a condom off the bed, tore it open, and slid it over Zack's rock-hard and probably almost painful erection. "Can you fuck me harder than Adam did?"

Adam shook his head with a laugh, impressed again with her boldness and not offended in the slightest.

Zack growled at the challenge in her eyes. "I guess you'll just have to find out." He spanked her hard, and she yelped. "Get that sexy ass on the bed."

She lay down on her back.

"On your hands and knees." Adam dropped his voice an octave for the command. As he'd hoped, her face flushed pink, and her chest rose and fell with quickening breaths.

She complied, arching her back so her luscious ass popped higher, ready for whatever they wanted to give her.

"Good girl," Adam cooed, stroking between her shoulder blades. She sighed softly at the well-deserved praise.

Zack knelt behind Kyla, slapping the side of her hip. She inhaled a startled gasp before grinding her ass against Zack's erection. "Mmm…" he hummed. "So ready to get fucked again, your body's begging for it."

"Don't make me beg." Her head jerked toward Zack. "Make me come."

Adam smiled, loving her dirty talk. It was almost a shame her mouth was about to full.

Kyla's eyes landed on Adam before flicking to the space in front of her, calling him over. He happily obeyed, settling in front of her with his back against the headboard. She stretched forward, capturing his lips with hers before he could stop it. The kiss started gently but quickly turned ravenous, his hands tangling in the dark waves of her hair.

What's one more?

Adam's lips were already sore, but he couldn't get enough of her mouth. "I could kiss you all fucking night." His head jerked back at the thought.

Whoa.

Where did that come from?

What the hell am I doing?

"But I…" he stammered, pulling back until his head knocked the wall. "I don't kiss after sex."

"Hmm…" Kyla's eyes narrowed. "I thought you said no rules. Sure sounds like one to me."

That earned her a wide grin—she had him there. If Adam stuck to his usual rules and stopped kissing her, the agreement they all made while their clothes were still on would be broken. He was a man of his word, and that wouldn't be fair to her.

He'd also said no strings, which might be even harder to stick to.

"Kiss me again, Adam," she whispered.

Hearing his name on her lips weakened his last shred of resolve. He hesitated for only a beat before slipping a hand behind her head and dragging her face to his. Kyla hummed with pleasure as Zack entered her from behind, her body surging forward and hovering over Adam's lap. She looked down, and he was already hard again. Just from kissing her.

What. The. Fuck.

It was a disappointment that she wasn't easy to shrug off, but also a relief because, in truth, he didn't want to stop kissing her. Hell, he didn't even want to watch her walk out his door when the sex was over. It was like she'd cast a damn spell that overrode the detachment that always made it easy to keep a barrier between him and women. Casual exchanges of bodily fluids was all he'd ever known.

Was he even capable of more?

"Suck him, princess." Zack's voice was low and strained with the need for release.

Kyla's gorgeous tits swung beneath her as Zack found his rhythm. She dipped her head into Adam's lap and took him into her mouth, moaning around his cock as she took all of him and his best friend at the same time. She matched the slides of her mouth to Zack's thrusts, the trio moving like a sweaty piston on its way to explode.

Adam trailed his hands from her shoulders to the small of her back before dragging them up again, his fingernails scraping her skin. Her responding moan vibrated through him, the buzzing tingle traveling down to his balls.

Kyla stuck her hand between her legs and slipped a wet finger beneath him, circling his anus. "Yes or no?"

Adam's lips curled up in a smirk. "No, but I appreciate the offer."

She smiled back and instead smeared her cream on his testicles, cupping them and giving a firm but careful squeeze, nudging him closer to the finish line. His pulse thudded in his neck, and she pushed his cock to the side and bathed his balls with her tongue, lapping off the wetness she'd left behind. This woman was a fucking treasure.

Adam grabbed her face and pulled her in for a kiss, licking and sucking her taste off her tongue like he was starving for it. He was—he was starving for *her*. And for the strange, floaty feeling she was giving him.

"Fuck, Kyla." Adam growled as she suckled the crown of his cock while Zack pounded her harder. "Just like that."

Adam's lips parted as he watched her. "The sweetest girls always turn out to be the dirtiest, don't they, Zacky?"

"And the most fun," Zack said, a sharp smack ringing out as he slapped the side of her hip.

Adam wrapped Kyla's hair around his fist and pumped his hips to fuck her mouth, her eyes going hazy and her features going slack. He knew that look. Women got it when they were overwhelmed by the sensation of being filled and used, freely taking and giving pleasure, and not feeling ashamed about enjoying every fucking second.

It was a beautiful thing, especially on her.

Unable to speak, Adam tapped her shoulder in warning, but her head shook, and she stayed on his cock. *A fucking treasure.*

Heat pooled low in his belly as the slide of her warm, wet mouth took him right to the edge. Finally, his muscles tensed, and he spilled down her throat with a rumbling growl that barely sounded human. Kyla's eyes remained fixed on his like she was savoring his reaction, soaking in the look of intense pleasure she'd put on his face.

When he was through, and she lifted her head, she wore the same satisfied smile as before. If she enjoyed having a belly full of his cum, he wasn't about to question it.

Kyla's eyes slid shut as Zack thrust harder, his hips slapping the skin of her ass in a relentless rhythm. "Sorry, Adam," she panted, "but he is fucking me harder."

Zack laughed. "Haha, motherfucker."

"But you're bigger." A wide grin stretched Kyla's face.

"What have you got to say now, *motherfucker*?" Adam laughed, and they joined in before Zack quickened his thrusts.

Kyla panted like she'd run a mile, clutching the bedding in her fists. "Fuck!" she gritted out. "Just like that."

Adam watched as a look of pure ecstasy bloomed on her face. "That's it, baby." As the pleasure pulled her deeper, her cheeks grew flushed, her kiss-swollen lips parted, and her eyes screwed shut. He tapped her chin. "Look at me. I want to watch it take you."

When her eyes opened, they stayed on Adam. He knew he was playing a dangerous game by watching her like this, but he couldn't resist. Her sky-blue irises sparkled in the light above their heads as she finally let go with a low, guttural groan that echoed in his ears. Her fluttering lashes were dotted with tears, but he knew by the broad, unrestrained smile on her face that they didn't come from sadness or pain. They came from feeling overwhelmed by pleasure. Kyla's blissed-out face was the most beautiful thing he'd ever seen, and he tried to convince himself that the tears suddenly clouding his vision came from the same place.

After three more thrusts, Zack grunted as he came and collapsed against her back.

"Fuck, I needed that." Zack pulled out and wiped the sweat from his brow as he caught his breath. "You're amazing, Kyla." He patted her hip, climbed off the bed, and headed for the bathroom. When the door shut, there was a snap of latex before the toilet flushed.

5

Adam

Kyla sat cross-legged on the bed, suddenly looking a little awkward now that they were alone.

"Still having fun?" Adam asked, an odd lilt to his voice that made him cringe a little. He sat beside her, the sides of their arms and legs touching.

"Is it stupid if I say this is already one of the best nights of my life?" Her nose wrinkled like she was self-conscious about the admission.

"Only if it's stupid if I say it's been one of mine too," he said.

Adam was a lot of things—immature, irresponsible, impulsive. One thing he wasn't was fake. He was honest and unafraid to speak his mind and share how he felt with people he trusted. His life and career were driven by passion and the freedom of letting himself get swept up in a song or a feeling that moved him. Why should this be any different? Because of self-imposed fucking rules? He wanted to know more about Kyla, and it would be stupid to pass on the opportunity to do that just because he was afraid of what it could lead to.

"Why did you decide to be a vet?" he asked.

It seemed like a good place to start. Their lives were different in so many ways, and he was curious about her passions.

Kyla smiled like she appreciated the question. She opened her mouth to respond, but a knock at the door cut her off. Zack came out of the bathroom and slid on boxers to answer it while Adam covered himself and Kyla with a blanket.

"Thanks, man," Zack said from the doorway. "Hey, what's $78.60 plus thirty percent?"

"$102.18," Adam and Kyla said in unison.

Her head whipped to him, her eyes wide. "How did you do that?"

Adam laughed at her shocked expression. It was probably the exact look he had after having his ass handed to him at *Mortal Kombat*. "Same way you did, baby. With math."

"But..." Her lips pressed into a tight line, probably biting back accidental insults.

Zack wheeled the cart of food in front of the bed and lifted the silver domes off the plates, the scents of French fries and greasy beef thick in the air. "He's done that shit since we were kids. Not as dumb as he looks."

Adam grabbed a fry off his plate and lobbed it at Zack's forehead. Direct hit.

"Numbers just make sense to me," Adam explained with a shrug. He didn't give two shits about history and couldn't write a book report with a gun to his head, but he aced every math class he'd ever taken. "So, why did you decide to be a vet?"

Kyla dipped a fry in her ranch and bit it in half. "I was the girl who always brought home stray cats and dogs. I'd sneak them food on my back porch and play with them in the backyard whenever my parents were too busy to catch me. I'd name them and love on them, even if they had fleas." She laughed, popping the other half of her fry into her mouth. While she chewed, her mouth remained closed, but it didn't matter anymore. He'd already accepted that there was no getting out of liking her. "Most of the time, my mom would figure it out and take them to the pound. I'd cry for days and do it all over again."

Adam thought about Charlie, the stray dog he'd found roaming the alleyway behind his family's apartment when he was ten. The dog wasn't wearing a collar, and his black fur was filthy and matted. Adam gave the dog a bath and carefully brushed out the knots the best he could with an old hairbrush. His parents let Charlie stay, and he and Adam were best buds for eight years until Charlie died of old age.

Adam's eyes stung with tears, remembering how badly it hurt to lose someone he loved so much. She probably saw people going through that pain every day. "Isn't it sad dealing with sick animals all the time?" He sipped his beer, struggling to swallow past the lump lodged in his throat. "And having to watch them die?"

"Sure." Kyla nodded, pressing a gentle kiss on his shoulder. The sympathy in her eyes made him wonder if she could read his thoughts. "But they still need someone to figure out what's wrong so they can be helped. They can't tell us where it hurts, so it's my job to gather the clues until I know what they need. If what they need is peace, I'm there to make sure they aren't alone when they find it. If what they need is a cuddle and a brand-new squeaky toy, I'm there for that, too."

Adam could only imagine the selflessness and compassion it took to do a job like that day after day. No one applauded her when she left her office or gave her shiny awards for what she did. Kyla saved lives. She eased pain and suffering.

Over the years, Adam had met a handful of rockstars he'd idolized since he was a kid, but he couldn't recall ever feeling the degree of awe and admiration he did right then.

As they sat there, basking in the afterglow and a connection that seemed to deepen with every minute that passed, he wanted to kiss her again. And again tomorrow. Maybe even for as long as he could before she saw sides of him she didn't like, got tired of his bullshit, and sent him back into the arms of faceless strippers, groupies, and any other beautiful and willing girl who was up for a few hours of fun.

It would be easy to imagine himself as the one getting tired of the same lips, same hands, same body, but Kyla had a sweet, genuine spirit none of the girls he'd been with before had ever had. Or maybe they did, and he was too busy maintaining his trusty wall between them to notice. But somehow, Kyla had figured out how to dismantle it brick by brick.

Of course, there was a chance his feelings for her were one-sided. As the thought sank in, Adam felt like a tub of ice water had been dumped over his head.

Maybe she still wasn't interested in anything more than a fun, casual three-some and some naughty memories to file away in her spank bank. Sure, she wasn't there just because he was a filthy rich rockstar like most girls would be. But she was there because he'd made filthy promises. That's what got her to that room. She knew his reputation as a player and said yes to the promise of sex with a guaranteed goodbye.

That most likely meant she still didn't want anything more, and he'd have to accept it—just like all the women he'd kicked to the curb over the years had to do. It was strange and uncomfortable being on the other side of that barrier. More than that, he actually felt guilty for ever making anyone feel that way.

Maybe the night would end in a big, fat, unexpected dose of long-overdue karma.

Once they'd finished their food, Zack went to grab his cigarettes from his room and have a smoke outside. Being alone with Kyla and a heap of uncertainty felt a little awkward until her soft, warm hand came to rest on Adam's bare thigh. Her fingers were inches from his cock, but this touch felt even more intimate somehow.

Kyla angled her body to face him. "Can I kiss you again?" she whispered, like she was afraid he'd say no. As if that would fucking happen.

Adam took her by the wrist and guided her into his lap, straddling his waist. "What is it about you, huh?" Warmth flooded his chest as he hooked an arm behind her waist and held her close. With the warmth came a sensation he couldn't name—like he was excited, terrified, and calm all at once. Their lips met, and he let the feeling—whatever the hell it was—soak into his bones while they kissed.

She drew back, brushing her lips to his. "Maybe you see a chance at something you've never let yourself have before."

Was she right? He could've had any woman he'd been with for more than one night, but he'd never seen the point. The sex wouldn't get better, the conversations felt pointless.

But it wasn't like that with Kyla. She was completely fucking gorgeous but also smart, compassionate, and fun to talk to. If she left and didn't look back, he'd be wondering about all the things he hadn't asked: What was her happiest memory? Did she prefer the mountains or the beach? What concerts had she been to? If she stayed, he could ask them all over breakfast. He could even tell her about himself, and not just the crazy tales of backstage debauchery groupies ate up. Real shit that actually mattered.

"I'm usually kicking the chick out the door by now, but..." Adam shook his head in disbelief, searching for the answer to the question that'd been poking at him all day—*what is it about her?*—as if it was written in her eyes. A sudden wave of nervousness made his muscles tense. The five words burning on the tip of his tongue might scare her off, but it was a risk he was willing to take because if he held them in, he'd never know. "I want you to stay."

"Really?" Her surprised gaze skated over his face like she was looking for answers, too. She relaxed in his arms when he responded with a nod. "I'd like that." She smiled and pressed her lips to his for a slow, gentle kiss. "Can we play some more?"

"You still want both of us?" A fresh wave of nerves prickled in Adam's chest at the question. He wouldn't feel right cutting Zack out, but even more, he didn't want to make her uncomfortable or feel pressured to carry on if she didn't want to. Knowing Zack, he'd be fine either way. He'd already come, so he probably expected to bail soon to crash in his room anyway.

Kyla hesitated before nodding her head. "Is that okay?"

He laughed. "It's all okay. Anything you want. There are no rules inside this room, remember?"

Especially after he'd broken all of his.

Her shoulders sank like she was relieved to hear it.

"We have a jacuzzi tub on the balcony," he said. "How does that sound?"

She smiled in a way that told him it sounded great before her words could. "I'd like that. Do you have any champagne?"

"In the fridge. Give me a sec." Adam kissed her cheek and fetched the bottle. He filled three glasses and handed one to Kyla before raising his own in the space between them. "To no fucking rules."

"You mean no rules for fucking?" She snickered at her wordplay.

"You heard me." He nudged her shoulder and laughed, sipping his champagne. The sweet bubbles fizzled on his tongue, mingling with the lingering taste of her. He walked onto the private balcony and started filling the jacuzzi tub, making sure the water would be nice and warm for the cold October night.

"Did you mean what you said?" she asked.

He turned to her with a question in his eyes as the steaming water rushed into the tub.

"That there's something special about me," she said. "That you want me to stay."

Adam exhaled a heavy breath, trying to find the right words. It wasn't easy since he'd never used them before.

Ever.

"Yes," he said finally. "It's strange, and I don't know what to do with it, but you're different somehow. I'm a dumb shit about a lot of things, but I know when a feeling's worth chasing." He leaned against the railing of the balcony while she stood in the doorway. The space between them made it easier to get his words out, but their eyes stayed connected. "Like when we write a song. Tyler comes with lyrics, and the guitar worked out, and I sink into the notes, trying to figure out where I fit. I work my sticks until I feel that charge that says I'm on the right track. I hit harder, test out beats and fills, and this *feeling* takes over. It says I need to keep going because there's a shiny pot of gold at the end of that fucking rainbow."

Her teeth sank into her bottom lip. "What feeling are you chasing here?" She gestured between them.

"I have no fucking idea." They both laughed, lightening the serious mood. "But I want to try to figure it out."

Kyla nodded, a soft smile curving her lips. "Me too."

Adam checked the tub, and it was nearly to the top, so he shut off the water and turned on the jets. He held out his hand, and she took it, climbing inside. He stepped in, sitting beside her and slinging an arm over her shoulders.

Zack walked through the sliding door, holding the third champagne glass. "Hell yeah, dude. Great fucking idea." Zack stepped into the tub, the tattoos on his chest and arms slipping beneath the water. A faint smell of smoke wafted over when he exhaled a long sigh of relief. "Having fun so far, Kyla?"

"Isn't it obvious?" Her smile grew. "And there are three condoms left, so I'd better have a lot more before the night is over. If you guys can handle it."

Zack chuckled. "Honey, I'm a twenty-six-year-old walking hard-on. I bet you'll tap out before we do."

"I guess we'll see," she said, her eyes smiling over the rim of her glass.

"Did you grow up in Portland?" Adam asked. That was another question he'd been itching to have answered.

Kyla nodded, the tips of her long, dark hair dipping into the water. "Yeah, and all my family and old friends are still there, so I plan to move back after my internship. Eventually, I want to open my own practice downtown."

It shouldn't matter that she'd be moving back to his hometown, but Adam was done with trying to place the usual limitations on whatever was going on between them. He filed the information away until he knew what to do with it.

"How did you guys meet?" she asked.

Adam sipped his champagne while lazily dragging his thumb over her collarbone. "First day of freshman year, I was walking home, and my lighter died when I was trying to light a cigarette. This long-haired freak sitting on the sidewalk in a Slayer shirt offered me his Bic."

Her jaw dropped. "You guys smoked when you were fourteen?"

Zack shrugged. "My dad's a clean-cut minister, and I was a rebellious shit."

"And I was a bored, stoner dirtbag," Adam said. "We dug the same bands, we both hated school. Match made in hell." The guys clinked glasses.

Kyla laughed. "When did the band start?"

"We met Tyler in detention a few months later," Adam explained with a wistful grin. "Zack and I were caught smoking behind the gym, and Ty got busted for carving a Black Sabbath logo into his desk. He was a band geek with awesome taste in music, so we all started hanging out."

Zack shook his head. "That boy was barely fifteen and could already fucking shred on guitar."

"It was wild," Adam said, remembering how blown away they were the first time they heard Tyler play. "We knew he'd make it. No doubt. We wanted to be part of it, so we snagged some cheap instruments at a swap meet and jammed in Zack's garage every day after school until dark. Eventually, it sounded good."

"Wow," she said, "I have to admit, I've heard *of* your band, but I've never heard your music."

Zack's eyes popped wide. "Been living under a fucking rock, lady?"

Kyla laughed, her hand finding Adam's knee under the steaming bubbles. "Basically. I busted my ass in high school to get scholarships. Then, my university coursework took all my time and focus. I've missed out on a lot of music that's come out in the last decade. When I do have time to zone out to a record, I usually go for classic rock."

"That's cool." Zack ran a wet hand over hair, slicking it back. "We're not for everyone."

"I saw the boombox in your room." Kyla's hand slid to the center of Adam's thigh and squeezed. "Can you play me something when we go back in?"

"Of course," Adam said, flattered that she was interested in their music. He'd be happy to play her something. As her fingers inched closer to his cock, he was looking forward to another round of sweaty sex that would come afterward.

He liked that she wasn't a fan. It was refreshing not to have to deal with the usual annoyance of women gushing over what songs they loved and begging them to play their albums as a soundtrack to the sex. He always went along with it, but it sort of made him feel used, and not in the fun way.

"Can I make another request?" Kyla asked.

Adam's champagne glass was nearly to his lips when she spoke. "Anything." He took a long sip of champagne as her hand crept higher up his thigh.

"Will you fuck me in the ass?"

Adam choked, sputtering out champagne into the water.

Zack and Kyla laughed while Adam coughed and wiped his mouth.

"Is that a yes?" she asked.

"Who are you asking?" Zack cocked an eyebrow.

"Adam's too big, so..."

Adam's head tipped back as he laughed. "I will *never* get tired of hearing her say I'm bigger than you."

Zack splashed him in the face. "If it means I get to fuck Kyla's ass, I'm glad to be just a *little bit* smaller. Half an inch, at best."

Adam scoffed. "Whatever you have to tell yourself, dude."

The guys laughed, and Kyla just rolled her eyes.

She sipped her champagne, licking tiny bubbles off her lips. "Would it work if Adam fucked my pussy at the same time?"

Adam loved hearing her ask for what she wanted without hesitation. This braver Kyla already had him half-hard again. As her hand continued its teasing slide between his legs, her knuckles brushed against his growing erection. She gave him a knowing glance, and her lips quirked.

"Of course," Adam said. "Have you had anal sex before?"

She looked at them both before shaking her head.

"*Fuuck.*" Zack's head sank back against the back of the tub. "An ass virgin? I'm in fucking heaven tonight."

"I've always been curious but never had the balls to ask for it." She stuck a finger in her cheek and made a popping sound. "There goes another cherry."

Adam grinned, his nose tracing her jawline and grazing her cheek. "Good thing I brought lube. You're gonna need it."

She lifted a brow. "You were pretty optimistic you'd find a hook-up at the reception, huh?"

He was. That's why he brought it along with the five condoms. But she wasn't just a hook-up. Maybe it started that way, but she wasn't anymore. The *why* was mattering less and less.

"I was hopeful," Adam admitted. "But I sure as shit didn't see you coming."

Zack's eyes narrowed as he watched them. "Something's up with you two. There's a vibe."

"A vibe?" Adam could see him trying to pick up on any silent communication Adam was putting down, but he had nothing for this—it was that unprecedented.

"Yeah, like you actually *like* her." Zack said the word like a curse, and she looked a little offended.

"Wow, thanks, Zack," she said. "Am I that hard to like?"

"No, babe." Zack's inked-up arms rested on the back of the tub. "But that's not what we do. We fuck, and we leave, or the chick leaves, but someone always fucking leaves."

"What if I don't want her to leave?" Adam asked.

Zack's eyes ping-ponged between them. "Okaaay. So what does that mean for the rest of the night?"

"Nothing changes with that," she said. "Can't I like Adam but still want you to fuck me in the ass?" She laughed, and they joined her. "You guys said no rules."

Zack sighed dramatically. "I guess if I have to."

Adam splashed him that time. "Ready for another round, party people?"

She nodded. "After you both play me your favorite Tomorrow Mourning songs, yes."

Kyla stood, water dripping down her bare skin and glistening in the dim light filtering out from the bedroom. For the first time, Adam took in the sight of the stars above their heads and listened to the sound of the waterfall and crickets down below. He'd been so distracted by her that he hadn't noticed any of it.

6

Kyla

Kyla stepped out of the tub and patted herself dry with a towel from the rack on the balcony. The guys dried off and followed her back into the suite. She yelped in surprise when Adam grabbed her waist and pulled her backward, her back crashing into his chest, which was extra warm from the heated water.

He wrapped his arms around her middle, and heat tingled low in her belly. She'd never been this free with her body. There wasn't a hint of her usual self-consciousness about her curvy hips or old playground scars as she stood naked in his arms. She let herself savor the heat of his firm muscles as he held her tighter. He was already hard for her again, and although she was getting sore, she was eager for more of anything they had to give.

But first, she wanted to listen to the music that was clearly as much a part of them as the tattoos etched into their skin.

"So," she said, "what song are you playing for me? It has to be your favorite."

Adam released her and grabbed a CD off the dresser. "I know just the one." He slid the disc into the stereo with a wide smile bursting with pride. "It's called 'Fade.'"

Kyla sat on the end of the bed buzzing with anticipation, eager for the music to start. Creativity fascinated her. She'd always gravitated toward math and science, and aside from having a decent singing voice and being pretty good at decorating cupcakes, she lacked any real artistic talent. The fact that someone's inner passions could lead them to create something out of nothing that was powerful enough to dazzle a legion of fans was incredible.

"Sappy shit," Zack mumbled, settling into the black leather recliner in the corner. "Ty wrote the lyrics after Charlotte dumped him. Life's so pointless and empty without love. Blah blah blah."

Kyla was glad her cousin decided to give Tyler a second chance because Charlotte had never been happier. And it was the reason Kyla was sitting naked in that suite with two equally naked and scorchingly hot rockstars who'd already rocked the hell out of her dull, tidy little world.

One had rocked it a little harder than expected, but she fully intended to roll with it.

Adam shook his head. "It's my favorite because it's the hardest to play. I practiced it so much before the last tour that my fucking calluses had calluses." He hit play and sat beside her on the bed.

Without thinking, Kyla laced her fingers with his. Guys like him probably didn't hold hands, but she did. Adam looked at their joined hands, and a corner of his mouth rose as the low thump of a bass kicked off the song. When the drums started, Adam's knee bounced, and his hand twitched in hers. As if his muscles took the familiar music as their cue to get to work. The guitar layered with the other instruments, but she focused on the drums. This was the song Adam had chosen to share, and it was easy to see why. His parts were the heartbeat backing up Tyler's words of heartbreak and Zack's low, relentless rhythm.

Kyla found her own knee bouncing to the beat, her head nodding along as all the other sounds disappeared, making way for a drum solo that sounded impossible for a human being to pull off. She smiled at Adam, in disbelief that she'd been in the presence of that level of talent and hadn't even known it. When the song ended, she exhaled a long-held breath.

"Wow." Kyla brushed her fingertips along the thick calluses he'd earned. "I can't believe these hands did that."

Adam smiled back. "You going to be a groupie now?"

She shoved him with her free hand because she wasn't ready to let him go with the other.

"My basslines were bumping there too, dammit," Zack said.

"You were amazing, too." Kyla turned to Zack before pointing at the stereo. "Your turn. Play your favorite."

Zack left his chair and stalked toward her. "Nope." His erection bobbed with his movements, and the sight of all the ink covering his arms and chest instantly made her wet. "I have a better idea."

Kyla knew what came next, and her mouth went dry at the thought of it. Maybe it was a mistake to trust two men she'd only known a few hours with breaking-in her backside, but she'd been curious for years. It was a night of trying new things, and she knew they were experienced enough to know how to keep her safe.

They'd only been rough when she asked for it, and they were careful with everything they'd done so far. Still, she was nervous that it would hurt.

"You'll be okay, I promise." Adam's hand slipped from hers as he got to his feet. Had her fear been that obvious? "But it's all right if you changed your mind."

Kyla shook her head. "I didn't. Just a little worried it'll hurt."

"I'll be careful and take it slow." Zack touched her shoulder. "You say stop, I stop."

"Okay," she said, her voice and hands a little shaky. "I trust you."

Adam smiled down at her before parting her knees and crouching between them at her eye level. "Good girl."

His words and the lust in his gaze sent a jolt of heat between her legs.

Adam leaned forward to plant a soft kiss on her lips. "Let me help get you ready for him. My cock might be too big for you, but my fingers aren't." His rough fingertips slid from her knees to the apex of her thighs, his thumb circling her clit. "Lie down on the bed."

Kyla crawled backward over the blankets on shaking limbs and did as he instructed. Adam grabbed something from the pocket of his suitcase, and when he got closer, she could see it was a bottle of lube.

"Help me get her ready." He tipped his chin at Zack, who responded with a knowing grin.

Zack sat near her shoulder and bent forward with his chest to her belly. His mouth moved between her legs, teasing her clit with his tongue. Her hips jerked, the tiny bead of nerves ridiculously sensitive after all the attention. As she rode it out, it started to feel good.

Adam lubed up his finger as Zack slid two of his inside her pussy. She cried out at the welcome but unexpected invasion.

"Fuck, she's tight," Zack mumbled against her flesh.

Adam circled her anus with his slick finger and slowly massaged her hole. "She sure is."

It was a strange feeling, but not in a bad way. Actually, when she focused on the sensation instead of the fear of pain, it felt really good. Adam's other hand stroked the outside of her thigh, silently encouraging her to let go of the last threads of anxiety that made it hard to fully be in the moment. Judging by everything else they'd done, this was going to be amazing. She just had to let go and trust.

7

Adam

When Kyla's tight ring of muscle started to relax, Adam slipped his finger in to the first knuckle. It was hard not to be jealous that Zack would be her first, but getting her ready was fun, too. He withdrew his finger before pushing inside again, a little further than before. "How does that feel, Kyla?"

"Weird, but in a good way." Her words were strained, and her eyes were closed, but she didn't look like she was in pain—just focused on adjusting to the new sensation. "It burns a little."

"That's okay," Adam said, stroking her thigh to help calm her. "It'll turn to pleasure soon enough."

A string of Zack's saliva mixed with her wetness slid onto Adam's finger, helping it slip in more smoothly. He got to the second knuckle and started sliding in and out, gently fucking her with one finger so she could get used to the feeling. Some girls decided this was too much and didn't want to go further. That was a good thing to figure out before things went too far.

"Still okay?" he asked.

"Yes," she answered with a stuttered whisper that said everything he needed to know without even looking at her face. "Please don't stop."

"Can you take another one?"

"I—I think so."

Adam lubed up a second finger and kept them close together as he slowly stretched the muscle until her body let him in. Her eyes opened, and she found his face. Kyla nodded, letting him know she was ready for more. He appreciated the communication and, even more, her trust. It meant more than she'd ever know to hear her say that she trusted them. And he'd be damn sure not to make her regret it.

After a third finger, she was panting and probably close to another orgasm, judging by how well Zack was working her pussy. Adam pulled out his fingers, and Zack stood. She grumbled in protest at the loss of attention, but she'd be happy again soon enough. Happier, even.

"You're good to go." Adam handed Zack the lube.

"No." Kyla propped herself up on her elbows as their heads turned to her. "Get him ready, too." Her eyes were on Adam when she said it, and he knew exactly what she wanted.

Dirty fucking girl.

Adam looked at Zack, and he got an *it's fine* shrug as a response. It was so hot watching Kyla get off that the night had quickly become all about making her coming wishes come true.

Zack put on a condom, and Adam squirted lube onto his palm before reaching for Zack's cock. Adam's eyes locked with Kyla's and her lips parted, her soft little breaths making her chest jump. His hand stroked from base to tip, concentrating a few short jerks just beneath the crown. He'd watched women give Zack pleasure hundreds of times, and that's what always made his eyes roll back in his stupid head. This time was no exception. Zack shut his eyes, probably imagining a woman stroking him instead of his best friend and bandmate.

"I cannot believe how fucking hot that is," she said, her fingers drifting between her legs as if she couldn't help herself.

Like Adam had said earlier, a hand was a hand. He didn't exactly get pleasure from the act itself, but witnessing Kya's reaction had him hard as steel. He couldn't wait another second to be back inside of her.

"Stand up." Adam released Zack's cock and slipped a fresh condom onto himself. He took Kyla's hand as she stood beside the bed. "Wrap your legs around my waist."

She hopped up and followed his instruction, hugging his neck and linking her ankles behind him. Adam gripped her ass cheeks in both hands, spreading her wide. The damp heat of her core pressed against him as he lifted her.

When he was positioned at her entrance, he pulled her down onto his cock, her slick heat letting him in with no resistance. Her breath hitched, her forehead falling to his shoulder. Adam used his grip on her ass to lift her up and sink her back down, fucking her slowly while Zack got into position behind her.

"Won't your arms get tired?" she asked, her voice soft and hazy.

Adam laughed. "I'm a drummer, baby. My arms don't get tired."

Zack gave him a thumbs up.

"You ready for this, Kyla?" Adam felt her nod against his shoulder. "We need to hear it. No shame in backing out."

She pulled back to look at him. "I want this. Just start slow."

The trust and raw vulnerability in her eyes made the burning feeling return to his chest. He kissed her and knew the second when Zack started to enter her from behind. Her muscles tensed, and she held her breath.

"Just relax, baby," Adam whispered in her ear. "Breathe and let him in."

Zack knew how to be careful, and Adam knew what signs to look for on a woman's face if it got to be too much. So far, Kyla was loving every second. And he was hooked on watching her as she adjusted to the feeling of being filled by both of them. She jerked in his arms, and a wince of pain crossed her face.

"You okay?" Adam tapped Zack's shoulder, telling him to stop.

"Yeah, just getting used to it. He's pretty big, too."

"Damn right I am," Zack said with a cocky smirk.

They all laughed, and Adam tapped Zack again to tell him to start again. As Zack moved, Adam sank deep. Kyla's eyebrows pinched, and she let out a moan that shot straight to Adam's cock.

"I'm all the way in," Zack said, his voice gravelly and edged with pleasure.

"I think she likes it," Adam whispered.

Kyla smiled, brushing her lips against Adam's. "Yes, she does." She gasped when Adam lifted her and slowly impaled her on both of their cocks. "Holy *fuck*. Don't you dare fucking stop."

The men worked together to fill her and fuck her until she screamed with an orgasm that might've woken the neighbors. *Fuck the neighbors.*

Zack was the next to blow, and he finished inside her with one last thrust that pushed her into Adam's chest. He held her tight as he chased his peak.

"You feel so fucking good after I come," she breathed in his ear.

That's all it took. Adam jerked his hips upward, and his head tipped back with a groan that made her legs squeeze tighter. When Zack slipped out and released her from behind, Kyla collapsed in Adam's arms. He carried her to the bed. Both men removed their condoms and flushed them. They shared an odd glance in the bathroom mirror, but Adam shook it off.

"Why do you flush them?" she asked. Most girls weren't observant enough to notice. Of course, it was already abundantly fucking clear that Kyla was definitely *not* most girls. "It's terrible for the plumbing."

"Because we're rich rockstars, honey." Zack ruffled his sex-mussed hair. "Can't risk some piece of backstage ass snatching it from the trash and knocking herself up to squeeze us for eighteen years of child support."

Her eyebrows shot up. "Women would do that?"

"Happened to a friend of ours," Adam said. "Don't take it personally, it's a habit at this point." He rifled through the minibar, found another water bottle, and held it out to her. "Drink this."

"How can I do that if my arms don't work?"

He laughed, sliding underneath her so she was sitting in his lap, his back against the headboard. He removed the cap and put the bottle to her lips. She took it from his hand and drained the whole thing.

"That was un-fucking-believable," she said with a heavy, contented sigh. "If you change your mind and want to kick me out, you're going to have to drag my devirginized ass to my suite down the hall."

Adam kissed the top of her head. "Your ass is staying right where it is." He could feel Zack's eyes on him, but Adam wasn't interested in whatever look of shock or judgment was burning into the side of his head.

"Shit," Kyla said. "There's only one condom left."

"Adam, can I talk to you on the balcony for a sec?" Zack aimed his thumb at the sliding glass door.

"Sure." Adam slid out from under her, dreading whatever bullshit he was about to hear. "I'll be right back." He kissed her temple and pulled a blanket over her before joining Zack outside.

Zack closed the door behind them. He looked at Adam, shaking his head with something like pity in his eyes. Pity for who wasn't clear. "Another one bites the fucking dust."

Adam backhanded his arm. "Don't be a dick."

"Don't be a dick?!" Zack whisper-screamed. "That's Charlotte's fucking cousin in there, man. She's a sweet little veterinarian, for fuck's sake. And you're a wild, perverted rockstar who can't keep his dick in his pants. What do you think's going to happen with a girl like that?"

A sweet little veterinarian? Hardly. Kyla had definitely proven there was a lot more to her than the shy, timid woman she first appeared to be. She was open-minded and adventurous, with a wild streak a mile long. And she knew who Adam was, yet she was still lying in his bed. She smiled and seemed excited when he asked if she'd stay the night. All of that had to count for something.

"I don't know, Zack. Maybe nothing. But I do know that if I act like an asshole and kick her out like I always do, I'll never know. I don't live with regrets, man, and I sure as hell don't want to start now."

"When it gets too hard to be miles apart, she'll bail."

Adam cocked his head, things making a lot more sense. "Like Mandy did to you? Isn't that what this is really about?"

"Fuck you, Adam." Zack raised his middle finger between them.

"No, Zack." Adam shoved his shoulder. "Fuck you! What if I'd given you shit when you liked Mandy? Would you have listened if I told you to back off? If you did, you would've lost out on the time you had with her. You'd never know what it was like to love someone other than your fucking self and your band."

Zack scoffed. "Look where it got me."

As far as they knew, Mandy still lived in Colorado, working as a club promoter/manager for Rollin' Rockies, a live music venue in downtown Denver.

Zack, Adam, and Tyler caught a show there when their band was in town on tour, and the second Zack met her, he was a goner. He took her on actual dates, held her fucking hand, and even brought her along to a few gigs. He tried his best to keep in touch after their tour moved on, but Mandy couldn't handle the distance and called it off.

Zack's pained expression made it clear that even ten months later, he still wasn't over her.

"At least you gave it a shot," Adam said, his tone softening. "You found out that you have what it takes to let someone in. Maybe it's my turn. If you fuck this up for me, I'll throw you over that goddamn railing." His lips twitched as he bit back a smile.

Zack held out his fist, and Adam bumped it. "It was a great fucking night, man."

"Our best yet," he agreed.

Zack's eyebrows raised, clearly surprised by that. Of course, it wasn't the best for him. He wasn't smacked upside the head with feelings he didn't even think he could have.

"So go in there and give it a shot." On the way back in, Zack clapped his shoulder. The silent communication said *it's all good*. They never fought for more than five minutes at a time and never held a grudge.

Zack grabbed his clothes off the floor and got dressed.

"You're leaving?" Kyla asked, sitting up in the bed.

"Yeah, last condom's all Adam's." Zack leaned over and kissed the center of Kyla's forehead. "So are you, if you'll have his crazy ass."

She smiled. "Thanks for everything."

Zack waved a hand. "My pleasure, princess. And please tell Charlotte and her dad not to kill us."

Laughter filled the room, and Zack walked out, the door clicking shut behind him.

Everything was quiet except for the faint sound of crickets outside the inn.

Adam stood by the bed, feeling awkward and unsure—more feelings that were completely foreign to him. "I've never done this before," he said, fiddling with the ring in his eyebrow.

"Done what?" She brushed a lock of hair off her face, studying him.

"Slept with a girl."

Her eyebrow cocked, a smile curving her lips that were puffy from all the action.

"You know what I mean." He sat beside her on the bed, keeping a little distance between their bodies while he adjusted to the situation. "I've never fallen asleep with a woman before."

"Wow." Kyla reached up and raked a hand through his hair. The gentle touch felt nice, helping to soothe his nerves. "How many cherries is that now? I lost count."

Adam laughed and kissed her again. He'd lost count of those, too. He grabbed her hips and slid her onto her back before moving above her, caging her in with his arms.

"Want me to grab that last condom?" He swooped down, taking her nipple into his mouth and releasing it with a soft pop.

"Yes." Her hands raked through his hair again, her beautiful blue eyes looking at him in a way that made his heart pound against his ribs.

Adam grabbed the condom and slipped it on. She was already so wet from the kissing and probably all the naughty new memories that he slid inside her tight heat in one smooth push.

They started off slow and easy, and he focused on the feeling of her soft, warm skin beneath him as their bodies connected. With his chest pressed to hers, he could feel her steady heartbeat fluttering beneath the surface. It kicked up when he kissed her and again when their gaze held, and they shared a silent communication of their own.

This time was different. Not just because they were alone but because it was clear they both felt something beyond what they'd set out to feel when their clothes first came off.

"Why did you say yes?" Adam asked, the motion of his hips stumbling a bit before he found it again.

Kyla brushed a few rogue hairs out of his eyes. "I thought about how free I used to feel. Before I made rules for myself that kept me from fully living. I wanted that feeling back."

Because of everything that happened since they met, he could relate. He'd made rules for himself that kept people at a distance and defined him in a way that'd become stifling. If Adam wasn't the crass, reckless playboy, who was he?

He'd become so used to that version of himself that he resisted change. Resisted fully living.

Not anymore.

"Free looks good on you, Bear Claw Girl." He planted a soft kiss on her forehead as he sunk deeper with long, slow strokes.

"You too," she said with a grin. "I'm glad I was brave enough to say yes."

Adam sealed his mouth to hers, savoring the feeling of their bare bodies moving together in a perfect rhythm. "So am I."

Her thighs squeezed his hips, and he swallowed her moan as she came. He wasn't far behind—with a few more thrusts, he let go, her inner walls squeezing and pulsing around his cock.

He held her close as their breathing slowed. Finally, he pulled out and tossed the condom in the trashcan beside the bed. He turned off the light, and they settled back in each other's arms. Kyla nuzzled into the crook of his neck, and Adam felt his own heart flutter.

Another first.

He breathed in the sweet cinnamon smell of her hair, exhaling with a sigh like he was releasing everything he'd held onto for too long—rules, limitations, the acceptance of loneliness. The fear of never knowing what real love felt like.

He'd watched his friends fall in love and become happier than they'd ever been. What was so crazy about wanting the same thing?

It would be ridiculous to use the l-word after just one intense night, but as Kyla rested against his chest, Adam felt a lot of things that seemed impossible only hours before. She saw past his surface bullshit and made him feel safe enough to let her in. It felt nice holding her as his eyelids grew heavy and his body relaxed. Even if things ended with her, just knowing he was capable of something bigger than empty sex felt like a victory.

"Adam?"

"Yeah?" He lazily stroked the hair at her temple.

"As soon as you fall asleep, I'm grabbing that condom and knocking myself up with your lovechild."

His chest jumped as he laughed, and Kyla snuggled closer.

"Then I guess I'll see you in court."

About the Author

Stephanie Louise has been obsessed with books since *Charlotte's Web* broke her heart when she was seven. Growing up, she wrote short stories and poetry, and now she writes spicy love stories that keep the pages turning.

Stephanie lives in the beautiful Pacific Northwest with her husband, two sons, and way too many crazy pets. She has a B.A. in English from Washington State University. When she's not writing, she's hiking in the rain, going to rock concerts, or cooking something loaded with garlic.

For updates, bonus content, and exclusive sneak peeks at upcoming releases, sign up for my monthly-ish newsletter on my website: http://www.stephanie-louise.com

Email: stephanielouisebooks@gmail.com

Instagram: http://instagram.com/authorstephanielouise

Facebook: http://facebook.com/authorstephanielouise

TikTok: http://www.tiktok.com/authorstephanielouise

Thank you SO MUCH for reading my books! Please take the time to leave a review. I truly appreciate hearing your thoughts, and it helps others find my work.